Choose your Lane to love!

Familiar Angel

"*Familiar Angel* is fantastic… a transcendent love story… Harry and Suriel are heroes to die for, and their love is a lesson … I can only have faith and desperately hope she will keep turning out more tales like this!"

—Cindy Dees, *NYT* and *USA Today* Bestselling author

Red Fish, Dead Fish

"The suspense is done so well, and the relationship between Ellery and Jackson is really engaging."

—Joyfully Jay

"Packed full of action, suspense, and of course steamy goodness, *Red Fish Dead Fish* is the sequel we have all been anxiously waiting for."

—Love Bytes

Manny Get Your Guy

"Amy Lane can tug my heartstrings better than any other author in the history of ever!"

—Hearts on Fire Reviews

"It's wonderfully sweet, and a perfect summer read. So, grab a towel (or a hammock!), pull up some sand and sunscreen, and while away an afternoon with these guys."

—The Novel Approach

More Praise for
AMY LANE

The Virgin Manny

"I have no qualms about recommending this one. In fact, I might just insist you all go get it."

—Joyfully Jay

Summer Lessons

"This read was a sweet and snarky romance with a whole lot of funny, dirty and sassy moments thrown in for good measure."

—Gay Book Reviews

"This series is a delight! If only we were all lucky enough to find such a wonderful group of friends."

—The Novel Approach

Tart and Sweet

"I highly recommend this book and the entire Candy Man series both in written and audio-book formats… 5+ Stars!! A MUST read!!"

—Alpha Book Club

"Amy Lane has done it yet again: Pure. F*cking. Magic"

—Diverse Reader

By Amy Lane

Published by DREAMSPINNER PRESS
www.dreamspinnerpress.com

By Amy Lane

JOHNNIES
Chase in Shadow • Dex in Blue
Ethan in Gold • Black John
Super Sock Man

GRANBY KNITTING
The Winter Courtship Rituals of
Fur-Bearing Critters
How to Raise an Honest Rabbit
Knitter in His Natural Habitat
Blackbird Knitting
in a Bunny's Lair

TALKER
Talker • Talker's Redemption
Talker's Graduation

WINTER BALL
Winter Ball • Summer Lessons

ANTHOLOGIES
The Granby Knitting Menagerie
The Talker Collection

Published by DSP Publications
The Green's Hill Novellas

LITTLE GODDESS
Vulnerable
Woulded, Vol. 1
Wounded, Vol. 2
Bound, Vol. 1
Bound, Vol. 2
Rampant, Vol. 1
Rampant, Vol. 2
Quickening, Vol. 1
Quickening, Vol. 2
Green's Hill Werewolves, Vol. 1
Green's Hill Werewolves, Vol. 2

Published by Harmony Ink Press
BITTER MOON SAGA
Triane's Son Rising
Triane's Son Learning
Triane's Son Fighting
Triane's Son Reigning

Published by DREAMSPINNER PRESS
www.dreamspinnerpress.com

FAMILIAR ANGEL

Amy Lane

DREAMSPINNER
PRESS

Published by

DREAMSPINNER PRESS

5032 Capital Circle SW, Suite 2, PMB# 279, Tallahassee, FL 32305-7886 USA
www.dreamspinnerpress.com

ISBN: 978-1-63533-945-1
Digital ISBN: 978-1-63533-946-8
Library of Congress Control Number: 2017910302
Published October 2017
v. 1.0

Printed in the United States of America

This paper meets the requirements of
ANSI/NISO Z39.48-1992 (Permanence of Paper).

Mate, Mary, and Karen. And Lynn for laughing at parts. And E for believing. And the kids for being patient with me.

ACKNOWLEDGMENTS

THANKS, MARY, because I only read a little bit of *Paradise Lost* in college and now I have three copies on my Kindle.

PROLOGUE

"EDWARD! FRANCIS! Are you here?"

Harry McTavish prowled around the clearing by the Sacramento River nervously. He'd barely managed to elude Big Cass, Golden Child's most fearsome enforcer, and his breath came fast in the chilly November night. Oh, of all the times to make their escape—but it couldn't be helped. Conrad Ames, railroad tycoon, gambler, terror of the brothels— even Golden Child, which catered to a specific type of taste—had finally set his sights on Francis.

Francis was barely fifteen.

Edward and Harry—they'd been around a year or three. Long enough to both have the pox, long enough to know their days were numbered. Harry's mother had died whoring at Golden Child, and Edward's had wandered in, delirious with pneumonia, a few years later, and they'd been bending over to stay alive long enough to feel a thousand years old. But Francis—he was young. Young and gentle. They'd spent the last two years protecting Francis, keeping him out of sight of the customers and Big Cass, making sure he had the jobs no one wanted to touch. Cleaning an outhouse was a filthy vocation, but it beat bending over and trying not to scream by a hot mile.

But Conrad had seen him, and Mistress Bertha would do anything to turn a coin.

Harry was the oldest. It was his job to protect the littler ones. That's what his ma had said before she'd died, after she'd managed to earn the coin to send his little sisters back east, to their gran. Didn't bother him that she'd had to do it on her back, and that he'd had to stay alive that way after. Fucking was just another trade, best he could see. But Francis's mother had died in the brothel, a used-up whore who had begged Bertha

1

to please, for the love of God, send her little boy to an orphanage, a relative, anything.

Bertha had promised her just so she'd shut up and die.

Harry and Edward had heard, though. Edward hadn't been whoring by that time, but they both knew it was coming, even then. Edward had the square jaw and lush mouth of a cowboy angel—wasn't a bugger on the planet who wouldn't have wanted to bend Edward over. Harry was plain and serviceable, but by then he'd learned to suck cock like a dream, because that way he got tips, plain and simple, and then the cock would be wet when it got shoved up his arse.

Together, they'd made a sort of silent pact to get Francis out of Golden Child before he had to clean more than toilets.

"Harry?" Edward sounded breathless and worried. "Harry—Big Cass almost got us." He burst out of the thicket of trees with Francis's arm over his shoulder, his body bearing the bulk of the weight. "Big Cass was right there. He clocked Francis a good one, Harry. He's out cold."

Harry swore and snarled—and kept his shiver to himself. "Goddammit all, we need to get out of here—*now*. The cargo train leaves at twelve. That's our way out of—"

A woman's scream stopped them in their tracks.

"Who?" Edward whispered, eyes wide.

"Hide!" Harry had just enough presence of mind to grab Francis's other side to help Edward pull him through the thicket of brambles that lined the river. Bleeding, dirty, breathless, they slid to a halt in a hollow between the blackberry bushes and the hill, lying on their stomachs, Francis sandwiched between them. Francis, who had received a terrible scratch from the corner of his mouth to the corner of his eye, moaned in pain. Harry shushed him, and Edward placed a gentle hand over his mouth.

A woman, clothed in blinding, glowing white, burst into the clearing with a man—man?—draped over her shoulder. His clothes were red velvet, and thick curly hair grew all over his face and large skull, like a goat's.

His back feet were cloven.

"Leonard," she begged. "Leonard… darling. Wake up. Wake up. I need your help."

Leonard—the thing... *man*—rolled his head, much like Francis had done, and moaned. "Emma, leave me. If they find me with you... if they find Mullins here...."

"Mullins!" the woman whispered. "Mullins—I'm losing him. Oh please—Mullins, he's losing himself again."

"I'm losing *myself* again!" came a terrible growl, and another Leonard-like thing stepped into the clearing—this one very obviously glowing red. "Emma, we need to do the ritual. I can't...." The monster thing, Mullins, let out a horrifying series of snuffling grunts and growls. "I'll turn," he said, sounding tearful—if a beast could be in tears. "I'll turn and gut you both."

"I understand," she whispered. "You've been very brave. Here." She set Leonard on the ground then and started to pull items from a leather satchel across her shoulder. "We'll do it right now."

"This isn't the ceremonial place!" Mullins said, sounding despondent. "It's not cleansed, it's not prepared—"

To Harry's surprise, Emma put a tender hand on the beast's cheek. "My sweet boy, you've been too long in hell. We don't need the trappings of the spell—although the things in those hex bags should help us focus. We just need ourselves, and our good intentions, and our desire."

Mullins's grunt was self-deprecating. "The road to hell is the one paved with good intentions," he said gruffly.

"That's only because the demons trying to get to earth walked that path first," she said, sounding cheeky. In their quiet interaction, Harry got a better look at her. Not young—over twenty—but not old either, she was beautiful in every sense of the word. Straight nose, even teeth, perfectly oval face, and blonde hair that streamed, thick and healthy, to her waist, she was what every boy should dream about when he went to sleep hoping for a wife.

Harry didn't dream about girls, but he could look at this one and know the appeal.

But it was more than the physical beauty—and she had it all, soft hips, small waist, large breasts—there was the kindness to the beasties. The gentleness and calm she radiated when Mullins had threatened her.

Suddenly Harry had a powerful yearning for his mum, when she'd been dead for nearly five years.

3

"Here," Emma said, breaking the sweetness of the moment. "Take the hex bags—there's ten. Make a pentagram with me and Leonard in the center. I'm summoning an angel, love. You may want to leave when you're done. I've no guarantees he'll be friendly to you."

"That's not news," Mullins said dryly and began his task. "Do you…. Emma, I know you're powerful. You summoned my master for knowledge on power alone. But all else you have done, you have done out of love."

"Including persuade you to our side," she said. While he set the hex bags, she was stretching Leonard out before her, stripping his shirt with deft, practiced movements. The skin underneath the clothes was smooth and human, and Harry felt nauseated at the abomination of beast and man.

But Emma seemed to care for him.

"It would be worth any torture," Mullins said softly, pausing in his duties, "to know Leonard will live."

"Come with us!" Emma begged. "I may not love you like I love Leonard, but you've been a good friend to us. Please—"

Mullins shook his head. "It's not enough to break me free," he said, and his bestial smile would haunt Harry and Edward for years. "Someone would have to love me enough to sacrifice for me, and make no mistake, Emma. This will come down to your sacrifice. You will be stripped of your power, your youth—are you sure you want to do this?"

Emma let out a sigh. "I would live a mortal lifetime without worry," she said softly. "But I do not want him all alone without me. 'Twould be cruel." She closed her eyes for a moment, and then—

Harry gasped and heard Edward do the same.

She was looking right at them.

"I'm about to do something very wrong," she said, great conviction carrying in her serenity. "But I think something very right too. Carry on, Mullins, but run as soon as you are done." Her voice dropped. "Please, my friend—I'll have enough weighing on my soul for tonight's doings as it is."

Mullins continued to bustle, and as he set the last hex bag down, Emma began to chant. Mullins traced a circle in the dirt around the outside bags, and then, when the circle ends touched, he pulled out a knife.

Emma nodded unhappily at him and then bit her lip as he cut a line on his palm and let the blood drip on the sealed ends of the dirt line. He and Emma looked at each other again, a strong friendship locking their gaze, before he turned and lurched away, his gait awkward and crippled on his cloven hooves. Harry felt some compassion for him then, poor beast, good friend—but his gaze didn't linger.

He was too busy watching the white light around Emma grow larger, filling the space inside the pentagram like a bowl.

The light exploded outward, filling the clearing itself, and then one more time, just a few feet more.

Harry and Edward stared at each other, terrified.

They were in the light circle as well.

"Glory!" Edward whispered, and Harry was too shaken to quiet him.

Francis stirred between them and opened his eyes slowly. For a moment Harry feared that he'd startle and scream—Harry certainly would have raised a bloody great hue and cry—but then, Francis wasn't Harry.

He parted his bruised lips and smiled.

"An angel," he breathed, and Harry turned his attention back to the center of the clearing.

Where an angel appeared.

Harry's heart stopped in his throat. Tall—because of course, right? An angel would be tall. Clothed in robes that glittered like diamonds, whiter than pearls he was. His hair was a marvelous flame-gold color, red like a sunrise or an ember. His face was more handsome than sin—bold, straight nose, full lips, a square jaw, eyes of warm, solid brown.

Harry's groin gave a painful throb, and he almost wept. Those things—those dirty, filthy things that were done to him by rough miners and haughty bankers with gold in their grubby fists—*those* things were not right here.

Not with an angel.

Not with *this* angel.

Harry's eyes burned with the perfection of this angel.

"Suriel," Emma breathed. Her voice held the same note of kindness, of friendship, that she'd had with Mullins. "How are you? Are your studies treating you well?"

Suriel looked away, and the face he turned toward the three interlopers in the brambles held such bleakness that Harry *did* weep. Not *his* angel, please. Not that despair for his angel.

"They are," he said, his voice resonant with a thousand church bells. "Emma, this thing you're doing—I'm not even sure God can make it true."

"Of course he can," she said, her voice rippling like water. "It's all about love, Suriel. And belief. Don't tell me all your laws forbid love!"

"I can't see anymore," Suriel said gruffly. "I am bound so tightly to every rule, to every law. Emma, I cannot even see my master's hand in the events as they unfold."

Emma dashed away a tear—but Harry let his fall.

"Then help me break this rule," she whispered. "I love him. I summoned him for knowledge, for healing. He was supposed to kill me—investigate my use of blackest magic."

"That's not what you practice," Suriel said, sounding puzzled. "You couldn't—"

"I couldn't talk to angels with a black heart." She smiled. Harry thought maybe she was much older than she looked—decades older. Centuries. "He learned that, in our time together. His protégé told me that…." Her chin wobbled, and for the first time Harry saw something besides serenity. "They suspected. His superiors suspected he'd been… tainted. He was supposed to bargain for my soul, and we spent hours just talking, with no bargain in sight. We…."

Suriel tilted his head, as though looking at something from a great distance. "You fell in love," he said, sounding surprised.

"We did." She dashed the back of her hand against her cheek. "His protégé and I barely got him away. Leonard was in my summoning circle, and the claws of the damned began to shred him. I pulled him and Mullins from the circle, and we were heading for the church, but—"

"This is your church," Suriel said, looking at the little patch of privacy in the wilderness. "I understand."

"I have the human power of sorcery, Suriel. Given me through my bloodline and decades of study. All I ask is for your divinity. We have the three of us here—divine, profane, and human, the mix of the two. We can cure him of his wounds—and set him free."

Suriel frowned. "You would give up your immortality?"

Emma bit her lip and winked, as bawdy as a dance house girl. "Now I didn't say that." Abruptly she sobered. "Now, Suriel—it needs to be now. A mortal is about to crash through our little church here—and not a nice one."

Harry and Edward looked at each other.

"Big Cass?" Harry asked, and Edward shrugged, nodding. Oh hells.

Suriel was cupping Emma's cheek. "I shall miss our talks," he said formally.

Her grin, bright and impish, spoke of such kindness. "We may still talk," she told him. "I won't lose it all in a rush. I'll be here for a while."

Suriel shook his head, and the stoicism, the worry that had beset the angel lightened fractionally. "Emma, I'm not even going to ask."

"Good." She sobered. "It's not altogether a heavenly thing I'm about to do. But I'm going to by God do it."

Suriel took her hands. "Shall we?"

Together they began to chant, a language Harry had only heard when he passed the Catholic church during mass. Their voices rose, then fell, then rose… then rose and rose and rose… reaching a pitched crescendo, leaving the air around them in the brilliant bowl of light, ringing like a bell.

The light grew too bright, the sound too great, too terrifying for mere mortals, and all three of the boys closed their eyes and cried out.

In an explosion of glory, they felt great things change about them—inside them, around them, and just when Harry thought his heart would stop with too much magic, the world around him went abruptly silent.

And then Francis and Edward meowed.

Harry spat and hissed, surprised, but Edward, a ginger tomcat with green eyes, sat abruptly down on his haunches and whimpered piteously, a lost kitten in the rain.

Francis—a cross-eyed Siamese—batted his paw in front of his eyes continuously, like harrying at an imaginary spider.

And Harry realized what had happened.

He darted out of the bramble bushes, hissing furiously, intent on ripping that woman's robes to shreds until she turned him and his friends *back*.

"Hush, hush, puss."

A strong hand grabbed him by the ruff and pulled him into equally strong arms. Harry struggled for a moment, but that hand, pulling at the fold of skin at his neck, oh, that was immobilizing.

But even more so was the strong arm wrapping around his body and holding him still—not cruelly, just… still.

He growled, anger a vicious turn in the pit of his stomach.

"Hello there, my little spy," Emma said softly. She was still on her knees by Leonard, who had… changed.

In place of the bestial head and cloven hooves were the long, plain features and big, clumsy feet of an average man. He groaned softly, and Emma whispered, "Stay still for a moment, my love. We have some things we need to do."

She stood heavily, and Harry got the feeling that, whatever she'd done, a great deal of her energy had gone into the result. Peering at her through his cat's vision, he saw that some of her brilliance had faded. She was still beautiful—and still glowing faintly.

"Welcome," she said softly, scratching him behind the ears. Harry hissed and batted out a black paw, but she dodged neatly. "Yes, you're our fighter, aren't you? I could feel you in the bushes, the three of you. You probably want to know what I've done."

Harry snarled. Oh, he knew what she'd done. He was a *cat*. He twitched his tail angrily, still growling, although Suriel's hand kept up an even, gentle stroking that soothed him in spite of himself. Being held kindly, firmly—this was a touch, a kindness, Harry had never experienced.

"I've made you my familiars," she said. Then she bent at the knees and called softly. "Puss, puss, puss… come to me, my pretties. We won't hurt you. Oh yes. Look at you, you handsome boys. Oh, our strong defender, kind and sweet."

8

Edward, you pushover! Look what she's done to us!

But it didn't matter. Edward sat stoically, accepting her scritches behind the ear with grave sobriety.

"And you. Oh… oh, so much affection."

Harry watched as Francis wrapped himself around her wrist. She picked him up—a delicate, small-boned cat—and he burrowed against her immediately, purring and nuzzling the crook of her elbow.

She smiled, a kind, maternal smile, and looked beseechingly at Harry. "I can give you a home," she said softly. "I can give you food and clothes. I can teach you to read and give you a purpose. I just ask that you hold my power, be my familiars, use my magic to change your shape and do no harm. I…." Her voice broke, and reluctantly Harry admitted that the poor woman had used a great deal of strength and so very much compassion in the few moments he'd seen her. "I just didn't want to leave him, you see. If I hadn't stored my power in the three of you, I would have aged and died right here, and he would have awakened in this world to live a long life alone. I'm sorry. I know it was wrong—so wrong—to not ask you. But please… won't you please forgive me enough to let us care for each other?"

Harry's growl ceased abruptly, and he melted into Suriel's arms in spite of his best attempts to hold on to his anger.

Strong arms—such a place of tender haven. For a moment, Harry remembered what it was like to be protected and loved. His heart bled and ached, and wed to Suriel's warmth…

It healed.

"She's very kind," Suriel told him, the words low and seemingly for Harry and Harry alone. Harry let out the cat version of a sigh and licked a line up Suriel's wrist.

In that moment of quiet, he realized the itching, the sickness he'd felt in his stones, his arse, his throat and gut was gone for the first time in a year. His lungs had been rattling—pneumonia, the pox, who knew?—but he could breathe free and easy now. He looked unhappily at Edward, who began to lick his paw philosophically, and looked again at Francis, who was begging Emma for more affection.

She could give them things Harry could not.

She could give Harry things he'd never dreamed of.

He turned his head and searched out Suriel's gaze. *I trust you. You're so beautiful, and you are holding me so safely.*

Suriel smiled and held out a smooth finger, devoid of human lines or roughness. Harry rubbed his whiskers against it anyway.

Please say you'll be there to guide us? Please, Suriel.

"Emma," Suriel said in sudden urgency, "there's a human coming this way. I can distract him, but you need to take Leonard and the boys to sanctuary."

Emma nodded and pulled Leonard to his feet with the hand not holding Francis. The very plain, very serviceable-looking human reached down humbly toward Edward. "Young sir," he said, voice formal, "may I carry you?"

Edward allowed himself to be borne aloft, and Suriel held Harry to his chest. In that moment, Harry was as surrounded by safety, by love, as he could ever imagine being.

"You'll walk on your own," Suriel said, a thread of humor in his voice. "You wouldn't have it any other way, would you, young master?"

Harry rubbed his whiskers against Suriel's robe and then pushed out of his arms to land lightly on the sparse grass of the clearing.

"Do you know where you will go?" Suriel asked urgently.

"The church first," Emma said, her earlier vulnerability forgotten in their need. "Then I have some train tickets to San Francisco. I do believe I shall be carrying some very unusual bags."

A part of Harry jumped excitedly. They were going to travel by train after all. And they didn't even have to stow away in a freight car.

Emma and Leonard started off through the trees, but Harry paused and turned around. Suriel had already begun peering in the opposite direction, looking for the approaching threat, and Harry was forgotten.

He didn't want to be forgotten.

He meowed imperiously, because dammit, how dare this man—angel—show him affection and kindness and then tell him to be on his way.

Suriel turned briefly. "Go, young master. I do not doubt we shall meet each other again!"

At that moment a familiar figure crashed through the woods, and Harry hissed. Big Cass, enforcer, bugger, hard-handed cock—he'd been the bane of the boys' existence for years. A shaft of terror shot through Harry's breast, and he chittered, simultaneously driven to attack and driven away in fear.

Improbably, he felt Suriel's kind hand along his back, soothing him, and he let a bit of fear and pain from previous encounters with Cass slip through his mind.

Suriel's howl of outrage shook the trees.

"Run!" he shouted. "An angel's justice is swift!"

Harry gasped and ran, but not before he saw, growing in stature and brilliance, Suriel's true form unfurling.

He was enormous and angry, a terrifying figure of retribution.

With a bellow, he raised his shining fist to the heavens and smote the burly, once-frightening body of Harry's biggest fear.

Big Cass screamed—and disappeared, the remains of his mortal flesh scattering across the clearing like thick crimson water thrown from a bucket.

At his back, Suriel vanished.

HARRY KEPT running, keeping Emma's soft glow a consistent light in the distance, and eventually he caught up. In the cold, clear dawn, she led the way quietly through the cobblestone streets until they came to a bare wooden door, a humble closet in the wooden facades of the Sacramento business district.

She opened the door, and they followed her down a flight of narrow concrete stairs and into a small room, surrounded by brick on all sides.

She and Leonard led the way, each of them holding their charge with utmost care, and Harry followed, even his lighter, healthy limbs growing weighty with exhaustion.

It had been something of a day.

When they got to the bottom of the stairs, they found a tiny bed— rope frame, clean-ish straw-ticked mattress—and a small bag filled with bread and cheese, with a water bottle next to it.

Harry sniffed curiously at the bag, and then… oh! Oh yes! He perked up and darted into the shadows—which were suddenly brighter and friendlier than he'd suspected. He'd seen cats do this a thousand times—with a bat of his paw and a crack of rodent neck, he had dinner.

He dragged it out—it was half the size of Francis—and dropped it at Emma's feet. He would try this maneuver later for a variety of people, and no one ever behaved as Emma did that first night.

She dropped to her haunches and smiled, stroking his neck, even while he emitted a low-level growling sound. "Well done, Harry. It will make my job easier if you and the other boys can fend for yourselves. Can you share this with them, you think?"

Harry's growl changed pitch, and even while he frowned to himself, Edward struggled out of the crook of Leonard's elbow and landed solidly next to him. With a sniff and a delicate lick of his whiskers, he chose a thick rat hindquarter and began to dig in. Emma set Francis down gently, and Harry pulled off a strip of skin to leave the tenderer flesh exposed.

She smiled. "You're a good leader, Harry. Thank you. If you three can refresh yourselves, I'll see to Leonard, and we can talk about what to do next."

The rat tasted… well, like food. Protein. Harry and the others ate ravenously, and Emma and Leonard sat on the bed and worked out details. Things like "inheritance" and "coast" were bandied about, and Leonard spoke in a quiet, dry voice that nevertheless managed to convey a great deal of absolutely besotted affection aimed at their mistress.

In the next hundred and something years, that tone never changed.

WHEN THE cats had eaten and the humans had cleaned up, they rested for the night before the boys jumped into Emma's carpet bag and Emma and Leonard walked—like respectable citizens—to the train station.

They had a car all to themselves, like royalty, and she held court there, talking to the three boys in their cat forms as though lecturing schoolboys in a hall.

By the time they disembarked, in a damp and sparsely populated place called Mendocino, the three of them had a pretty good idea of what their lives would be.

They held Emma's power—not all of it, but enough. Enough to keep them all, Emma and Leonard included, young, aging slowly at roughly a rate of five years every hundred or so. They'd age faster if they spent most of their time as humans, slower if they spent their time as cats.

The boys would pick up on small spells—escape, communication, protection—as they studied with Emma, and they were free to use the spells in moderation.

Emma was very frank with them. Their livelihoods depended upon cooperation. If the boys grew greedy for power, Emma and Leonard would wither and die, and the things Emma could teach them, could give them as they grew, would be no more.

If Emma and Leonard were cruel masters, if they were unfair in the things they asked of the three, the boys could opt, at any moment, to simply live as humans, take their chances, and leave the rest of the collective to struggle on, considerably weakened.

Harry turned into a human at this, dismayed to find that none of the dirt or the ragged clothing he'd worn had disappeared or changed in the twenty-four hours he'd been a cat at this point. "But does that mean we can't leave *ever*?" he asked unhappily.

"Not at all," Emma said. Her hand—elegant and small-boned, although her nails were broken under her gloves—moved automatically toward him, as though to pet and soothe. Before Harry knew what he'd done, he'd turned cat, and she smiled as she followed through on the motion. "Stay with us, young Harry," she said, her eyelids fluttering shut as she leaned into Leonard's strong chest. "We'll keep you safe. We'll give you a harbor in this stormy sea of a world. And when you're ready, I'll divest you of the spell and you can go out and make your way as a man, and we can be friends. But until then, please—please consider what this arrangement can do for *you*."

Edward and Harry would talk about it in the years to come, about how they would know they were ready to move on. Francis never did. Francis stayed cat so often, he hardly spoke as a human. He kept to himself, fragile, secretive, dependent, for the next hundred and forty years. His home was in Emma's and Leonard's arms, and he clung to them, even as a boy.

But Edward and Harry wondered—when would their turn come? When would they have done with family entanglements and a binding to a family they'd stumbled upon in a clearing?

Harry wasn't sure when they stopped talking about leaving and started talking about how to stay forever. He kept waiting for the sweetness of Emma's maternal nature to fade, for the insistence of work, of repayment for all her kindnesses to fall upon their backs.

It never did.

They disembarked in Mendocino, and Emma reported immediately to the land office. She had, nestled in the mountains near the coast, a large bit of property with a cabin.

The cabin had a living area with a wood stove for cooking and a few wooden chairs and a table, as well as a small bedroom—mostly room for a mattress, resting on top of a dresser which was just wide enough to use as a frame.

No sooner had Emma and Leonard burst in through the door than they got to work.

Cleaning, cooking, chinking the corners of the cabin against the cold. Sewing new blankets, ticking cushions for the chairs, hooking rugs for the floors, building shutters for the hole in the wall that served as a window.

The boys stayed huddled at first in the center of the cabin, watching the two humans work competently and cheerfully, explaining what they were doing as they were doing it.

Then Harry saw a spider about to drop onto the back of Leonard's neck, and in a smooth leap and catch, he pinned the thing to the ground.

Leonard turned his angular, homely face to him then and said, "Protecting me, Harry? I'll take some help if you're interested."

Harry had changed then, and then Edward, and while Francis stalked spiders and mice—an important task, nobody argued—the two of them worked as humans alongside Emma and Leonard.

Emma would bring in water from the stream nearby and allow the boys to bathe.

Leonard traded Emma's hoarded gold for leather and nails and made them sturdy boots for when they were human.

By the time true winter rolled around, all three boys could walk into town as boys and be clothed and shod the same as every young man in the tiny township.

They didn't go often, but Harry told Edward and Francis that it made him feel like a king.

During the cold hours of the winter, Emma read them stories by oil lamp as they curled on her lap as kitties. Genies and lamps, beasts and merchants' daughters, angels falling from heaven—even disillusioned princes traveling into the world and returning home to mourn their innocence. She allowed their playful paws to follow her fingers on the page.

They learned to read.

The cabin expanded, amenities were added, more rooms.

They learned carpentry at first, and plumbing, and then, as time furthered, gas and electrical skills.

Emma bought books from far and wide. Leonard became a physician, helping the people in the small township, telling folks Edward was his son. Edward would grow just a little bit older as time went by, so the townspeople didn't get suspicious.

Sometimes, in their studies, Emma would call Mullins or Suriel. The angel and the demon became as dear to the boys as they were to Leonard and Emma—but only Harry wandered the cliffsides alone after Suriel's visits, looking off into the sea as though it would glow bright with red-gold hair and sober brown eyes. The angel always made him feel safe beyond words when he filled the house with light, but when he disappeared, Harry felt the closest thing to grief he ever hoped to weigh down his heart.

That grief would grow subtly in the years to come. Harry never noticed when he stopped looking forward to Suriel's visits and started wondering how he would fill the empty hours after them.

But between visits, they fought, they laughed, they played, they worked, they studied—they loved like family, with a kind mother, a gentle father, and three boys who chose to study as often as they chose to go romping through the wildflowers in the warmth of June.

The outside world passed them in its whirl and blur, except for the odd occasions of Edward and Harry going off into town sometimes, seeking companionship, looking for lovers.

It wasn't until Harry took a young boy who had lost a limb in a war to his bed that Harry even asked where he'd been in battle.

The answer was Flanders, and that was how the family learned about WWI.

They endeavored to learn a little more about the world, but it wasn't until Edward, who bedded both boys and girls, came running into the house—there were more than eight rooms added to the original cabin by now—with a tearful brothel girl in tow that the boys found their purpose.

One that burned fiercely in the heart of everybody in the family, as it turned out.

It would become sort of a family business.

Hanging by a Thread

Dammit, Harry, call him!

Harry grunted and labored at the wheel, working hard to haul four tons of freight truck around a corner without tumbling himself, Edward, Francis, and the girls locked in the back all over the on-ramp from Bakersfield to I-5.

You okay back there?

Telepathy—that had been the three familiars' favorite spell, and they'd never regretted the time it took to study.

It's a bit rough, Francis said diplomatically, and Harry grimaced. "It's a bit rough," from Francis, meant—

In the name of seven hells, Harry, they're scared enough already! You're rattling their teeth from their heads!

Dammit, Edward, I'm doing my best! They'd traveled down to Bakersfield on the word of one of their spies—a particularly observant crow. Seymour was not the most empathetic of witnesses—he tended to look at people in terms of "not dead yet," "mostly dead," and "lunch"—but he did know human behavior well enough to spot trafficking in a hot second.

And he lived for Emma's baking. She'd make him bread every day for a month if only he could give them reliable information.

Harry and Edward had driven while Francis had curled up in the comfortable bed in the back of the cab, but once they'd arrived at the filthy storage facility, baking in the sun, his languor had disappeared.

Francis had never sold himself—but Harry and Edward had figured out that he'd experienced so much evil in the brothel that he hated the place, the institution, with a more than frightening passion. In the nearly hundred and forty years since they'd dragged him away from Golden Child in escape, he had yet to take a lover. His body had aged—not

17

as much as Harry and Edward, who looked to be in their late twenties now—but still, he could pass for twenty-one if pressed.

But his soul seemed as young, as fragile and untouched, as it had that wondrous, terrifying night.

And his fury to rescue those trafficked and imprisoned as human cattle was a brilliant, all-consuming light, second only to his devotion to Bel, Leonard and Emma's son.

Bel was the focus of all the family—they petted him and spoiled him with all the considerable love in their hearts. It was hard for the three familiars to leave their happy little clearing and what stood now to be a mansion, tucked well back from the cliffside and against the trees.

But there were over fifty girls in the back of the semi Harry was driving, and as the iron behemoth jounced down the crumbling stretch of freeway, Harry could only be glad Beltane Youngblood was back in Mendocino, preparing to leave for Oxford in the fall.

Francis had been their advance guard, sneaking into the stifling storage room when one of the guards had opened it up to shove in buckets of tepid water and empty other buckets full of waste.

Francis didn't talk to the girls—because, coming from a cat, that would have scared them to death—but he'd hidden in a corner and projected serenity, kindness, and hope.

Enough so that when the guards had left and Harry and Edward were able to bust the lock on the door and roll it up, the girls didn't fight—and weren't frightened—when the boys ushered them into yet another semitruck, this one full of clean clothes, food, soap and water for washing, and bottled water for drinking.

Francis and Edward had gone with them, Francis as a cat and Edward as a man. Edward had been their best linguist as the years had gone, so he spoke to them in Russian and Spanish by turns, telling them it was an escape and doctoring the ones who were hurt.

And Harry got to drive.

Harry *loved* to drive.

But he was not quite as fond of it when people were shooting at him.

Right now there were four battered vehicles—transport vans and SUVs—full of unwashed musclebound assholes shooting at the truck.

Edward, keep them down!

No kidding! Francis has a shield around us, but it's only so strong!

Shields were hard—Harry couldn't do one, and Edward could only project a little bit of radio interference. Francis could do the most complex spellwork of any of them, but he didn't work well under pressure.

Harry spotted an off-ramp ahead, relatively empty, with an overpass that actually led beyond a series of hills to his left. He had no idea what lay over the hills, but the road wrapped around them, and hopefully he could shake these guys there.

Or at least push their cars off the road, which would help a hell of a lot.

Hold on!

The off-ramp was on his right, and the turn over the overpass was at an acute angle the other direction. By all rights, the mass of the truck should have pulled them over. But Harry focused his will and lifted—*hard*. The truck didn't fly necessarily, but it did lift up enough to balance itself on the road instead of flipping in a leviathan tangle of twisted metal and pulverized flesh.

He heard Edward's *Oolf!* in his head but was concentrating too hard to respond to his fear.

What he knew would happen—but hoped wouldn't matter—was that the cab of the truck, running now at right angles to where the bad guys were disembarking on the off-ramp, made a perfect target.

The first flurry of bullets caught the door, but they were fired wildly from a distance and his luck held. The second flurry of bullets from the next jeep in line was a little closer—and one of them punctured his luck.

And his shoulder and his lung.

Dammit!

Oh Jesus, Harry—call him!

I can still drive!

His body exploded into a giant painflower, but he kept both hands on the damned wheel. He'd been hurt before—a knife in the ribs in Monterey, a serious beating in Las Vegas, and a solid shot to the stomach in Portland—and he knew how to keep functioning. There was enough magic among the familiars and Emma and Leonard to keep him from dying, even from a mortal wound, and if he could just hold on for a bit, grit his teeth and growl through the pain, he could get his brothers and their charges to safety. Edward could heal him then—healing was Edward's specialty, like defense was Francis's.

They didn't need to resort to drastic measures.

More shots, all of them wide but still dangerous, and Harry pulled in as much air as he could and gunned the godsbefucked semi. The road dropped suddenly and then rose, and he was damned if he was going to lose any momentum if he had to weave through two minivans and an SUV to do it.

He made it through without touching any of the innocent vehicles in his way and stood on the accelerator to pull the truck through the first grueling hairpin turn.

He could actually *hear* the girls scream in the back of the truck, no magic telepathy required, and he silently begged their forgiveness. The back end of the truck lifted up, and he used his magic to fight it back onto the road. The tires caught, and his heart started beating again, but sluggishly as the blood poured thickly from his shoulder and chest.

He could fight his way through the haze of pain, but dammit, he was having trouble breathing.

Harry, if you don't call him, I will!

No—please. It hurts him so much.... But Harry was fading, he could feel it, and the next turn of the road was coming. Two of the jeeps were passing him on the wrong side, against the rail, guns blazing, and Harry gave the wheel a yank. The truck skewed, and the jeeps were smashed through the rails and rolled down the side of the hill, bodies flying out as they went. Harry barely noticed because he was fighting the wheel so hard to get it back online. Oh, dammit... dammit... he couldn't breathe anymore... couldn't see.... The truck swerved, and the front wheel broke free before he wrestled it back onto the road.

Oh God. He was going to get his brothers and the innocents in the back killed.

Suriel, I'm sorry. I'm sorry, but I need you—

A brilliant flash of light materialized next to him, and Suriel's hands, bright and shiny and clean, entered his vision, taking the wheel from him.

"Oh, Harry! You're dying again! Why didn't you call me sooner?"

"Didn't want... hurt you." And the blackness behind his vision finally won. As he slumped behind the wheel, Suriel's warmth surrounded him, and he could smell eucalyptus and green tea.

EMMA AND Leonard and their three familiars had lived in the little cabin in Mendocino for nearly twenty years before Harry figured out the cost of calling Suriel.

By then each of the boys lived in his own room and had a bathroom to share, and Leonard had introduced running water and a small electric generator run from a windmill they built on the cliff.

Emma summoned Suriel perhaps once every two years, based on need. Once it was to help teach the boys healing spells, and once it was to discover a language spell that could allow them all to learn languages they'd never heard. She usually waited for a peaceful night, one during which all the boys were excited about their studies and had saved up questions to ask.

Harry loved the nights Suriel came.

He stood while the boys ranged around him in a careful circle, their heartbeats taking the place of the powerful hex bags Emma had used before. There was no blood used in this spell—no demand. This was all about courtesy. "Suriel, our friend, our wise scholar, our compassionate angel, can you come and converse with us this fine night? We will be respectful of all discourse and generous with our faith."

Those were the actual words of the spell Emma made them memorize, and Harry—who had yet to learn the knack of poetry or languages—secretly treasured every syllable.

He would never forget the safety, the feeling of belonging that night when he'd curled up in Suriel's arms and Suriel had taken a moment to comfort a strange animal and an even more bewildered human being.

On this particular night, long after the others had fallen asleep—Edward and Francis curled up in contented purring balls, Emma and Leonard dozing on the couch nearby—Harry had kept Suriel long past the allotted time, asking him questions. Why were the stars bright? Why were humans subject to disease? Would the rest of the world someday have the seemingly magical things Leonard had brought to their home with engineering and education?

Suriel answered every question patiently, with kindness, and Harry sat cross-legged in his position on the floor, eagerly keeping the angel there for as long as possible.

Finally the night wound down, the candles lit for the summoning guttering in their stands, and a pregnant quiet settled between them. Harry looked longingly at Suriel's angel-bright face and realized the vague impression of inhuman beauty he'd gotten that first night had changed subtly in the years that passed. Now those features had refined themselves to a pleasing narrowness, a square jaw, an almost piquant chin, wide-set gold-brown eyes, and that glorious reddish hair.

Harry didn't want to fall asleep, because then he'd have to stop glutting himself on the beauty of Suriel.

"Now, if *all* of your questions have been answered...." Suriel's lush mouth quirked at the sides, as though he were very aware that Harry had been stalling.

Harry's heart pounded in his throat. "One more," he begged in a whisper. "Suriel, why are some people attracted to their own sex, like me, and some people attracted to both, like Edward, and some people to the opposite, like Leonard and Emma?"

Suriel's eyes widened. "Because that is how you were made," he said simply, and then a profound sorrow crossed his features. "It was not supposed to be a painful or a confusing thing. God made the mold, but humans added their own spices—"

"Like how Emma flavors the meat with garlic and Leonard just uses salt and pepper?" Harry asked, needing to be clear.

"Yes. Exactly. And sometimes things get a little muddled in the process. There are women whose genitalia is male, but their hearts are female, and men who are the opposite. That is the human part of the equation—and there will surely be a human solution."

"That would be hard," Harry said, thinking unashamedly about his cock and how much he'd learned to enjoy it in the past twenty years. They'd spent five years, at the least, hearing Emma talk about how there was no shame in any kind and enjoyable thing their bodies did before the memories of the brothel faded enough for them to enjoy the pleasures of the flesh.

"You like your body?" Suriel asked, and on the surface it was an affectionate interest that drove the question, but Harry heard something deeper throbbing beneath the angel's voice, and his heart warmed.

"I like it very much," he confessed with a grin. "In the brothel, all the touches were… ownership. I was meat. But Emma told us our bodies were our own—they should feel good." He could feel his expression turning sultry and hoped there was no sin in talking of such things with an angel. "I like feeling good, Suriel. I like it a lot."

Suriel's throaty laughter was the sweetest reward for his candor. "I'm glad you feel good, young Harry. That is as the God and Goddess intended." Suriel spoke sometimes of the Goddess, but he'd managed to neatly dodge any questions about her, and Emma didn't press.

"What about angels?" Harry asked—never subtle, not Harry. "Are they allowed to feel good?"

A look of profound sorrow crossed Suriel's features—but that wasn't the worst of it. Suriel began to speak, and as the words came, a terrible network of slashes, as though from a glass-studded whip, opened up on his face, his arms, his chest, his thighs.

"Angels fall," Suriel said softly, his voice quivering with pain. "Not the great fall of Lucifer and his followers—I'm talking smaller. Usually, they fall in love with someone or something in the mortal world, and they come to earth. Their immortality and brightness fall away, and for a mortal moment, they walk the world as men and women, and their lives are their own for a lifespan before they ascend to the heavens again."

"Suriel! Your face—"

"Some of them bond to their humans, and their humans ascend with them, or they are reborn together, to find each other again and again."

Tears began to fall from his eyes, lovely sparkling diamonds dropping gently onto the horror of bloody stripes, appearing and healing on his flesh.

"Can you do it?" Harry asked, appalled by his suffering, hurt to his core. "Can you leave your bondage to a God who would do this to you?"

"Oh my boy," Suriel said, his sorrowful smile wounding Harry worst of all. "I am the Angel Who Is Bound. It is my *job* to suffer for all of those bound to service against their will. Every moment I spend with you and your beautiful family is a joy to me—but always, always there is a price."

Harry was sobbing by now. "Oh, Suriel—don't. Don't do this if you're to be tortured for it!"

"But staying away would hurt me most of all."

And with that, the last of the candles blew out and the first bit of sunlight shone through the window. Suriel disappeared, leaving a small puddle of actual diamonds in the center of their summoning circle, where his tears had fallen.

Harry turned cat as he'd faded out of sight, and he stayed that way for the better part of a year. Finally, Emma pried the story out of him.

"We can't call him anymore." Harry wept on her as he'd rarely wept, even in the early days when his heart had been so sore from his use in the brothel that sometimes he couldn't breathe. "We can't—we can't."

"It would hurt him worse," Emma said softly into his dark hair. "He wouldn't come if he didn't love us. Sometimes, if we love someone deeply enough, we'd endure a thousand tortures rather than stay away." Her face softened. "I stopped summoning Leonard when I realized he was being tortured in hell for speaking to me. But he missed me, you see—began to appear to me in dreams, just so I could tell him about my day."

Harry nodded and wept more into her shoulder, but he listened. He'd never thought of love before, until he'd seen Emma and Leonard, working together, pulling together to build a life and to parent the three motherless boys they had included in their circle by accident.

But he'd spent twenty years by this point seeing how a couple functioned, listening to them argue and knowing that when the argument was resolved, they would make love. Emma and Leonard had things to teach him about being human that he'd never fathomed as a child, and he would not turn from that learning now.

"What made you call him?" Harry asked her, his voice raw.

"I wanted to interact with him," she said, laughing softly. "I wanted to see his expression unclouded by the filter of sleep. I needed him so badly, I had to trust he was telling the truth when he said he was glad to be with me, no matter what the consequences. Sometimes that's all you have—trust that you are enough."

Harry eventually stopped weeping, and he turned cat a little less often as the year passed. And when the time came that Suriel's guidance was needed once more, he didn't object to the family calling him.

He even stayed up late again, to talk to Suriel one-on-one, to enjoy his company.

Suriel thanked him as he faded, saying the private moments with Harry made his appearance worth the pain.

So Harry had achieved some peace with their angel, a way to accept the affection he so obviously bore their family without drowning in guilt and self-inflicted pain.

But as the family business had changed, grown more dangerous and purpose-driven, he'd been forced to call Suriel more often—and each time he thought it hurt the angel worse.

The first time had been the beating in Las Vegas.

Edward and Francis had gotten away with the girls—and a few boys—but the mobsters who ran the prostitution ring had caught Harry, who'd been the last one out of the building.

Harry told the boys to go on without him and to come back when their charges were free, thinking he could stall, could hold out, could manage about anything the mob goons dished out in the meantime.

The beating had begun, and he'd held tough—but when his ribs had broken, puncturing his lungs, he'd thought longingly of Suriel and how he'd never see the angel again.

And Suriel had appeared.

Harry remembered that moment, the golden light of benevolence and kindness washing over him, Suriel's voice rocking him to his core, the fury cushioned in Harry's ears by Suriel's intent.

The mobsters had dropped to the ground, screaming, their ears bleeding with the scream of an angel protecting his family.

Harry had passed out then and awakened healed and naked in the desert, Francis and Edward drawing near, frantic because he'd dropped out of their telepathy for an hour. Suriel had delivered him—from torture, from death—and then disappeared without a word.

Harry knew he was loved as a family member, but he mourned for what Suriel must have endured to love him.

He vowed to call Suriel as little as possible after that.

Suriel, on the other hand, seemed to just appear when Harry needed him most....

"HARRY?"

Harry was in someone's arms, somebody strong who smelled like eucalyptus and tea. Harry had taken lovers over his lifetime—but never for long. A flirtation, a feeling, a moment encased in glass—those things he could live with.

Giving his heart to someone—committing beyond his family—that was not a thing he could live with.

Emma had explained very carefully. Choosing a mortal lover meant one of two things. Either the familiars could give up their powers and live as mortals did, or the familiars could live with their lovers but watch them grow old and die.

Emma and Leonard were the only home Harry had known. Francis, Edward, and now Bel—they were the brothers he'd forged from his heart. He'd never give them up for a fancy or a flirtation.

But this... this was quite different.

This wasn't a fancy. This was a cornerstone in the bedrock of his soul.

"Suriel?" he mumbled. "What are you still doing here?"

The hand over his brow soothed him, lulled him away from his agitation. "You were very close to death, Harry. I'm not ready for you to die quite so soon."

Harry's dry chuckle made no sound. "I'm nearly a hundred and sixty years old, Suriel," he corrected, still finding it hard to breathe. "I should have died of the pox before I was twenty. Every minute after that is a gift."

Soft lips brushed his forehead. "You should never die, Harry. You should be young forever and ever. And loved, so passionately, so thoroughly, that your soul is greedy for one last touch of your lover's soul."

Harry smiled, lost in Suriel's poetry as easily now as he had been in his youth. "I've yet to find a lover like that. I'm beginning to doubt they exist."

"Someday you must."

The sadness in the tone was unmistakable. Harry struggled to sit up. "Suriel, where are we? You usually disappear after you come. Why are you still here?"

"We are in the middle of the fucking desert!" Edward said rudely from somewhere over Suriel's shoulder. "And he's still here because you came closer to death than ever before and Francis and I were coming unglued."

Harry smiled wryly at Suriel. "He's exaggerating," he said, just for Suriel's ears. Edward *sounded* like the most reasonable one of the three of them, but he was also—in Harry's words—their worrier princess. Edward could prophesy doom better than any supernatural being Harry had ever met, and then he'd produce the facts and figures to back up his prediction. The fact that he was wrong 80 percent of the time didn't seem to bother him. He insisted that was just because Harry would defy death to make sure Edward was only right once in a blue moon.

But Suriel didn't smile back as he sometimes did. "No, Harry. We need to give this one to Edward. This was as close as you may ever come again. I'm not sure I can make it in time to save you the next time."

Harry struggled to sit up, looking away. "I'm sorry, Suriel. I didn't mean to worry you." He looked around and frowned. "We really *are* in the middle of the fucking desert, aren't we?" They were gathered around a campfire, and as he looked out, he saw five other fires just like this one. Each fire had a group of girls huddled around it, holding their hands out to the flames in spite of the mild night.

Safety, Harry thought. They'd sweat where they stood if the fire would help them feel safe.

27

About fifty yards away, looking as out of place as a fish walking on its fins, was the semitruck, sitting serenely under the purple stars.

"That is unexpected," he understated. "How—"

"Suriel," Edward said grimly, and Harry frowned again, looking around. About three campfires away he saw Francis, weaving sinuously between the girls' ankles. Harry could see the aura of peace and sleep he was weaving as he sauntered, and he let out a sigh of relief.

Then he turned to Suriel. "How could you!" he chastised. "You must be in agony!"

A faint shadow flickered across Suriel's features. "No more so than usual," he said. "It was necessary."

"But why are you still—"

"Because this is my last mission with you."

Harry gasped and held his stomach. "I'm sorry?"

Suriel stood and helped him up. He peered into Harry's face and brushed his cheek with a knuckle. "Nothing to be sorry about, my boy. I am… I am at a tipping point, you understand? I can either stop my visits, or I can endure trials to come down and live among the humans." He swallowed and glanced out at the flickering fires and the gradually relaxing bodies of fifty human beings who had been bound against their will. "I can watch you all from heaven." His voice went soft as velvet. "There are other angels who can help you." The smile he turned to Harry was bitter as chocolate. "Angels you won't have to worry about hurting until you are at the point of death. I'll keep a good watch for you, Harry. I won't let your family down."

"But… so now…?"

"I'm here for one last adventure. If I decide to return, it's to be my gift, you see, for accepting my bondage like a dutiful angel. I get to work among you for a while—a short while—and then I must go." *Or suffer torture to stay.*

Harry gaped at him, hearing the unspoken part loud and clear, wondering if he'd been shot again. His mouth opened and closed, but no sound came out, and Suriel simply walked away, cutting a wide circle around the large encampment. Harry could read the weavings of crystal light he left in his wake, and he recognized a protection spell.

"Go?" Harry said numbly as Suriel's body became just a celestial glow against the purple velvet night. "He needs to explain 'go.'"

Edward appeared at his shoulder, square jaw tight, red-blond hair shorn above his collar and allowed a few inches on top. "He means he'll be up in heaven and we'll be down here until we die, moron. It's how angels and humans normally work."

Harry bit his lip, trying to breathe past the pain. "I… I… no Suriel? Why…." But he knew why. Suriel had just told him. Suriel was becoming human—too human. He would never be able to fulfill his duties if he continued to help the Youngbloods. "How…."

"How do we stop him?" Edward asked, and damn him. He loved Suriel too—all the family loved him—but he sounded puzzled, and reasonable, and all the things Harry was not.

Harry wanted to pound a fucking creosote bush until Suriel stopped this bullshit and things went back to normal.

"Yes," Harry whispered. "How do we stop him?"

Edward squeezed his shoulder then, his friend, his brother, his companion for nearly a century and a half. "There's two ways this can play out, Harry. One is that we take however much time Suriel is down here among us and convince him that falling is worth the trouble."

Harry swallowed. He hated this plan. "I'm not sure it is," he said, his throat sore. He loved his life in Mendocino, and he loved his adventures here on earth. But sometimes, when he curled up into a little ball of fur on his bed at night, his heart ached with loneliness. He'd been cat long enough to know he wanted a human companion, someone to stroke his fur, to rub his whiskers, to scratch that one place on his ruff.

He'd been human *just* enough to know he yearned for a lover, but more. Not a brief moment of pleasure, of skin on skin, but something longer.

Something that combined the two feelings.

Something he'd had only a few times since that moment in a clearing, a hundred and forty years ago.

"Well, the other way is for you to join him in heaven," Edward said, voice hard. "And I'm sorry if this bothers you, Harry, but that is unacceptable. So you had better just find a way to convince him to stay."

Harry glared at him. "I'm not suicidal, if that's what you're saying."

Edward grunted. "No, not suicidal—just damned transparent. Start looking at your own heart, my brother, and we can stop looking through Suriel to see it."

Edward started to stalk away, and Harry glared at him. "Edward—Edward, what am I supposed to do?" Usually they planned together, but their situation here was fairly unusual.

"Go hunt," Edward said shortly. "Everybody's hungry, and Francis is busy calming them down. A few jackrabbits, a deer if you can find one. Suriel said he saw grazing land—a park or something—a few miles to the south. Make yourself useful, but *don't* get hurt!"

Harry felt the sort of dejection that only came from being at odds with his brothers. "I don't get hurt on purpose," he said, trying a playful smile.

"Not on purpose," Edward replied. "No."

He turned away again, and Harry opened his mouth. "But—"

Edward held up his hand. "Harry, please. No more. Just be careful is all."

"Sure, brother," Harry said softly. "I'll be back periodically and leave the game outside each circle."

He changed form before Edward could answer and trotted off into the night.

Oh, he loved the darkness and the desert. The hills of the central valley had such interesting smells—cows far away, jackrabbits close up. The flora was different, tough succulents, the occasional creosote bush or scrub pine. He smelled the soft earth and watered grass two miles to the south, as Edward had promised, and set off in that direction, whiskers quivering in hope of game.

Ah! That bush to his right shook, and he looked at it sideways while he continued, his pace even, to trot southeast. And it shook again.

He veered a little—still south, but southwest this time, as though he just leaned a little to his right.

The leaves trembled, and Harry was too excited to hold himself together. He turned, smooth as a ball-bearing pivot, and darted into the bushes, claws out, teeth bared. Ah, it was a big one, plump and juicy, and it took a heave and a snap of the jaws to break the poor jackrabbit's neck.

It was still twitching as he dragged it back to the campfires, choosing the circle he'd awakened in, apparently the one the men were using, so as not to frighten the women. He dropped the jackrabbit, feeling smug, and turned back into the night, kicking a little bit of earth across it as though to say, "I am done with this, and it's your turn now!" He hadn't taken many steps when the glory of light that came from an angel stopped him.

"Did you bring us food, Harry? How thoughtful." Suriel squatted in the dirt and extended his finger. Harry nosed it delicately, and then a little harder, and then a little harder. When Suriel started scratching him behind his ears, his back end grew a mind of his own, and he flopped to his side in the dust, glutted on the affection of the one the person he'd always craved it from the most.

Suriel chuckled. Something about Harry in this form gave them their easy friendship again. No awkwardness, none of Harry's guilt or yearning to spend more time with Suriel, none of Suriel's underlying sadness or pain.

Harry started batting his fingers, all play, and Suriel tapped him on the nose. "Now, I could stay here and do this all night, brave Harry, but I don't think that one jackrabbit is going to feed all these people."

Harry swished his tail and stood up, kicking sand at Suriel in a snit and starting off into the night again.

"Harry," Suriel called. "Wait. I can come with you."

Harry turned to him, puzzled, just in time to watch as Suriel turned from a humanoid man with spectral wings and a lot of inner radiance into a… a… a cat.

A long-haired ginger—a Maine coon cat, if one ever existed with long, flowing hair the color of Edward's. He was enormous, a good four feet long and nearly two feet at the shoulder.

For a moment, Harry just stared at him, dazzled, until Suriel cuffed him gently with a massive paw.

Oh yes. They were going *hunting*.

Harry gave the air a little sniff and then led the way, back from where he'd come, toward the parklands with the green and growing smells.

And the deer.

Suriel hunted like a dream. He glided, he charged, he pounced, all a fluid melding of spirt and muscle. Harry worked as the distraction. While Harry was sauntering around their prey, drawing the deer's wary attention, Suriel snuck in behind it and leaped, bringing the animal down with a quick bite to the spinal cord and a crack to the neck.

They didn't stop at one deer, but kept hunting until three of them lay bleeding by the stream that fed the small park.

When they were done, Suriel extended his powerful claws and very neatly eviscerated each animal, while Harry dragged the offal slightly away from the water so scavengers could have their way with it. When he was done, Suriel looked at him pointedly and then gestured imperiously at the stream.

For the first time since they'd changed form, Harry felt compelled to use telepathy and actual words.

Really?

You're covered in blood. Wash it off.

So are you!

Suriel looked down at himself and startled.

What? Harry asked. *Angels don't get bloody?*

Well, not usually, no.

Harry changed form and glared at him until Suriel did the same.

"Not usually?" Harry asked, not bothering to strip. His clothes were just as bloody as he was—they would both need a good long swish in the water. "What does that mean?"

"It means that usually my… my *glory*, I guess, takes care of the human parts." Suriel sounded worried, and now Harry worried too.

"Does that mean—you're not human yet, are you?" Oh God— seriously, *God*—please don't let Suriel get stuck down here, in this prison of loneliness that defined the boundaries of Harry's heart.

Suriel thought about it and then smiled. "No. No, I still have a ways to go. I think this is just… a lesson, you see? A reminder of the things I would need to worry about if I decided that I wanted to tip all the way over."

"Well, lesson learned," Harry said with deep disgust. If he didn't have to haul the deer across the desert, he'd be happy to just lick himself clean as a cat. But they needed to get the deer back to the fire in the next hour or so if the girls were going to eat before dawn.

Harry was about to jump into the water—as chilly as it was—when Suriel gave a snort. "We'll chafe if we walk back in wet clothes. Strip."

"The clothes will need washing," Harry said with a roll of his eyes. "The girls won't be any more excited about seeing men in bloody clothes than they would be about seeing us naked."

If he'd been another man, Harry would have sworn Suriel made a "dammit" face—but that couldn't be. What reason would Suriel have to see Harry naked?

"If we wash as cats, will the clothes wash?" Suriel asked, genuinely curious.

"Yes," Harry said, feeling patient. "Yes. Which is why I was just going to lick myself clean."

Suriel appeared to think about it. "Well, how about we strip and get in the water, then put on the clothes and turn, and then turn back after our fur is dry?"

Harry stared at him, genuinely puzzled. "Because why?"

Harry had never seen Suriel with a nervous tic before, but he had one now. He bit his lip in every appearance of embarrassed indecision.

"Because swimming under the starlight seems like a lovely thing to do and this may be my only chance," Suriel said in a rush, and Harry caught his breath.

Curiously he looked around, recognizing the quiet of the desert, the beauty of the stars overhead, the myriad life-forms teeming at the spring.

"Hunting was good, wasn't it?" he asked, feeling that moment of delight again that came from watching Suriel in motion.

"It was joyous," Suriel said sincerely.

"Then, if this is… is a thing you wish to do before you return, I say do it." He grinned then, stripping his T-shirt off over his head and his cargo shorts and boxers down his legs. He laughed shortly, because he was wearing hiking boots, and he had to stop, bare-assed naked, to unlace them, but he was done quickly and then looked to see if Suriel was ready to leap into the stream.

Suriel hadn't moved—was, in fact, staring at Harry with his mouth slightly parted and his tongue resting on his bottom lip as though he was studying something.

Harry gave him part of a smile. "Uh, Suriel? You, uh, may want to—"

Suriel had taken to wearing modern clothes when he appeared before the family. His wings were always present, but they simply… were. An extension of his body. Clothes, ceiling, walls, just seemed to part to accommodate them. Today he was wearing a leather jacket, white T-shirt, jeans, and motorcycle boots. He slid the jacket from his shoulders and pulled off his T-shirt while toeing off the black leather boots, and there was suddenly not enough oxygen in the world.

Long body, defined chest, enough muscles in his stomach to make it ripple perfectly, and arms with firm bulges in all the right places, smooth, shining golden skin… in one heartbeat, two breaths, three blinks of the eye, Suriel ceased to be a sexless angel and became a very handsome, very desirable, very *male* being, and Harry's heart crawled into his throat and tried to strangle him with its beating.

The boots flipped off, and Suriel stepped out of his jeans and boxers, and Harry's whole world stopped.

It wasn't just that he was well-endowed—although he was bigger than any mortal Harry had ever lain with—it was that he was… perfect.

Hips, waist, thighs—oh dear Lord, even his knees were sexy—and of course that great swinging half-flaccid cock growing along his thigh.

Suriel glanced up, his brown eyes taking in Harry's speechlessness, and he smiled, an almost decadent, wicked expression.

"Do you enjoy what you see?" he asked innocently.

Harry had to swallow twice to answer through a rough throat. "You're beautiful."

Suriel's eyes hooded. "You are too, Harry. I've never seen you naked before."

Harry's groin tingled, and his balls swung heavily by his thighs. "I'm, uh…." A hint of a breeze hit the tip of his erect cock, and he shivered.

He was already dripping.

"Water," he mumbled, turning and jumping into the spring.

Oh no—that was a mistake. The rill was fed partly from an irrigation ditch and partly from a natural spring. The water from the irrigation ditch ran clean and cool, but the spring was heated. The water was like a summer bath, refreshing, but after a moment it was only a few degrees cooler than the blood that thundered through Harry's veins.

His erection was not getting any smaller.

He heard a splash and turned to watch as Suriel plodded delightedly deeper into the rill. At its deepest the water stood only chest high, and every step seemed to fill him with new sensation.

Harry couldn't help it—they had people waiting on them, waiting on the spoils of the hunt—but he'd never been so entranced by another person's pleasure.

"Your first swim?" he asked, smiling.

"It's glorious." Suriel relaxed, floating on his back, his arms and legs spread under the stars. Harry laughed gently and closed his eyes. The water lapped at his skin, and although his arousal hadn't calmed down, he fell into the moment, the chirping of crickets under the bushes, the furtive sounds of rabbits and possums moving beyond the reach of the two deadly predators who had just turned human and jumped into the spring.

He opened his eyes, and Suriel stood nearby, looking at him fondly through the darkness. "You look happy," he said, sounding satisfied. "All this time, Harry—I'm not sure I've ever seen you happy."

Harry blinked at him, a frown marring the moment, but he couldn't help it. "I'm happy at home," he said, brows drawn together. "I'm happy reading with Leonard in the study or helping Emma cook."

Suriel shook his head sadly. "Do you think I haven't looked in on you then?" He reached out with a gentle finger and traced the ridge where Harry's brows drew together. "You have this line then too."

Harry bit his lip, feeling strangely vulnerable. "I'm just trying to—"

"Trying to do what they tell you," Suriel said softly. "Obedience has never come naturally to you, Harry. Perhaps you shouldn't try so hard." Again, his finger traced a delicate path over Harry's face, and Harry caught his hand briefly.

"I'll try not to be so obedient," he rasped, "but maybe we should take the deer back to Edward first. They need to be cooked too."

Suriel nodded—and then moved his finger back to Harry's brow. "Yes," he murmured. "But I have one more thing I'd like to do. It's something I've wanted to do for quite some time, brave Harry. You wouldn't deprive me of it now, would you?"

Harry's mouth parted, and his heart beat in his throat—and his groin.

"No," he whispered. "I'd give anything for you, Suriel. You know that."

Suriel stood some inches taller than him—they'd never been this close. He'd never realized how helpless he'd feel before the angel of his salvation.

"It's a simple thing, really." A tiny smile pulled at the corners of Suriel's lush mouth. "But it's all I've wanted for quite some time."

He lowered his head then, and brushed his lips against Harry's in a simple kiss.

Harry gasped, raising his hands to Suriel's bare shoulders, and at the feeling of that smooth golden skin under his palms, he moaned and leaned closer.

For a breathless moment under the heavens they were skin to skin in the silken water, and the kiss deepened. Suriel tasted glorious, filling Harry's mouth, making him drunk and greedy. He opened and allowed Suriel inside, clinging tightly, wrapping his legs around Suriel's thighs, winding arms around his neck.

Suriel cupped his bottom, pushing them closer, and the feeling of his erection, rubbing against Harry's, almost sent him spiraling, rutting, spilling his climax into the saguaro-scented water.

Suriel pulled back, resting his forehead against Harry's. "We," he said deliberately, "will finish this later."

Harry let out a sob and buried his face against Suriel's neck. "What is this?" he asked, shaking with want. "What—why are you— Suriel, I'm lost."

"I'm falling," Suriel whispered in his ear. "Let's find each other, just not—"

"Now." Harry had a job to do. "Not now." His family had dedicated the past century to saving people who had been just like Harry, Edward, and Francis. Harry couldn't let them down now.

Any of them.

They took a deep breath, and then another, and Harry unlocked his legs, shuddering at the loss of Suriel's bare skin against his. His feet had just touched bottom when a sound—a familiar sound—broke the silence of the watering hole.

"Shit!" Harry swore. "Suriel—we need to go!"

"I'll get the game," Suriel said with surety. "You get away."

Before Harry could ask how—even as a large hunting cat, Suriel couldn't haul three small deer—Suriel had changed again, this time quite spectacularly.

Where a man had stood, desirable and warm, a giant golden eagle with a wingspan the size of the watering hole lifted out of the water. With a shriek it grasped the three deer in its still-dripping claws and pumped its mighty wings to rise up into the sky.

Harry could have watched him fly forever, his freedom and glory a beautiful ache in Harry's heart, but another bullet whizzed by, frighteningly close. Harry ducked under the water and swam for the edge, turning cat as soon as he reached it. He heard shouts of "Where'd he go!" and "Dammit, did you get him!" as he trotted out of the water, and with one last lingering look over his shoulder at his boots, he ran back into the desert.

He paused as he got to the grassy edge and crouched under a creosote bush to see where their attackers were heading.

A solid figure, shaved bald, with a great bushy mustache, thundered out of the darkness, and five smaller figures also dressed in black orbited around him, asteroids around a corrupt moon.

Harry's first instinct was to cry out, but even as a cat, that could be fatal. His second was to hide—crawl inside the heart of the creosote bush and never come out.

His third instinct—the one he obeyed because his family needed him—was to stay exactly where he was and listen. And watch. And see if this was who he thought it was.

"Not one of you whoresons hit what you were shooting at?" The man who looked exactly like the nightmare from Harry's youth turned and spat into the earth. Harry almost expected the sand to steam.

"That was unnatural," hissed one of the smaller men. "Was I the only one to see—"

"Nothing." The speaker, a withered, hunched man, looked furtively over his shoulder and made the sign of the cross. "You saw nothing. They got away."

"What?" Big Cass—because that was the only way Harry could think of him—asked suspiciously. "What did you see? I was in the back, looking for the others. What did you see?"

"First of all I saw faggots kissing, but that's no news." The man sneered at Big Cass. Cass cupped his groin and thrust, sneering back, and the man kept talking. "But we shot—and I swear, Cass, we got the big fucker. But the bullet just seemed to bounce off his back, and the next minute he was a great bloody bird!"

"There was a light!" the man next to him protested, sounding hysterical. "A great bloody light. Blinded me. When I could see again, they were both gone, and the dead things at the water with them!"

"Sure," the first man agreed resentfully. "A light. A whatever. It wasn't right!"

Big Cass chuckled, low in the pit of his stomach. "A big light? A man that's not a man? That's...." His chuckle grew bigger and uglier, and if Harry hadn't had urgent business to attend to, the first thing he would have done was vomit up the last thing he'd eaten. "That's the best news I've heard in a hundred years."

Then men around him laughed uneasily, like he was telling a joke, and maybe to them, he was.

But as Harry turned and skittered soundlessly into the night, he knew it was the least funny thing he'd heard since he and his brothers had hidden in a thorn bush and watched an angel heal a demon in response to a sorceress's tears.

FLYING

HARRY WOULD never forget the first time Emma and Leonard fought.

Leonard was a soft-spoken man, humble, with a dry sense of humor, and at first the boys had been puzzled as to how the two souls would find their way together when Emma was so warm, so passionate and fearless.

For the first few years, the boys were cats almost constantly. They learned to read as cats, their paws gliding softly along Emma's ancient tomes and their claws sometimes puncturing the paper. They slept together, tangled up, in the first year, a pile of fur at Emma and Leonard's feet, particularly when it was cold. If Emma and Leonard were making love, the three of them prowled around the outside of the cabin, guards against an intrusion that never came.

After two years of turning human maybe once every two months so Emma could trim their hair and they could shave what beards they grew, Leonard told her very firmly that they were forgetting their words and needed to be human more often. Perhaps once a week, he said, to sit at their table and converse. He'd built them a room by now, with beds of their own, but they still slept, a sinuous contortion of fur and muscle, at the humans' feet every night.

Harry had been napping behind the couch. Francis preferred to nap *on* the couch, and Edward usually chose a sunspot, where he would lie on his back and indulge, but Harry was a corner cat. He liked being snug and warm, with only one direction to look should danger threaten.

But Francis and Edward were off stalking mice that day, and Harry—who had been up late studying, still hoping then that the books would hold the secret to the loneliness he tried so hard to conceal—was hidden from view.

"No!" Emma snarled, "I will *not* tell them they must!"

"Emma, this isn't healthy for them. They were *boys*—nearly men—and I swear, Harry growls when he eats. The last time he sat at our table, he picked up a chunk of meat in both hands and growled. If we don't take them in hand, they will end up not quite sane!"

Harry kept his eyes deliberately closed, so if he was discovered they would think he hadn't heard. But inside he was alert, curious—and embarrassed. He hadn't realized he did the cat-growling-eating thing as a human. It was like sitting at the table naked, actually.

Beyond the couch he heard the sound of the broom being wielded across the hearthstones with unnecessary force. Emma was cleaning, which she did when agitated.

"Do you have any idea what their lives were like?" she asked angrily. "*Any?*"

"Yes, I was there when you met them, remem—"

"They call out for help in their sleep! Do you hear that?"

"Of course I do! Cat, human—they're running from Big Cass and the terrible things he did to the boys who were working—"

"Francis too!" Emma said, her voice breaking.

Harry's eyes shot open—Francis. They'd worked so hard to keep him safe.

"Did he tell you that?" Leonard asked softly. Francis had barely spoken to Leonard as a cat *or* a boy in this last year.

"Finally, yes. Apparently that man raped all of them, the boys and the girls—he was their 'breaking in.' Edward and Harry thought they'd gotten Francis out before it happened, but he'd been caught, just before the escape." Her voice broke. "He can't even think of a man's touch. A woman's either, but that's not who he'll desire. They're broken, Leonard. How can I make them sit at my table and demand silly human parlor tricks like eating with a fork and a knife—"

"Because they *are* human," Leonard snapped. "They aren't our pets, Emma—"

"Do you think I don't love them like my *sons*?" she cried.

"Do you think I don't either?" he yelled back. "They're sons, like Mullins was to me. And they are so grateful to be here, to be safe, to be protected—they're afraid to be young men because they're afraid they didn't learn it right—"

"And they're afraid of what will happen to them as young men," she added, voice passionate. "If they find safety in the guise of house cats, how can we rip that away from them!"

"Because they'll forget," he said softly. "And they'll never learn to trust us, sweetheart. How can they trust us if they never sit at our table and converse with words? You didn't bind them as familiars to rob them of their humanity, Emma—but if you don't start making them *be* human, that's exactly what will happen."

"Every night," she said, voice breaking. "One of them calls his name in their sleep *every night*."

"Even Harry," Leonard said sadly.

"Why?" Emma practically pounced. "Why is it so odd that Harry would call out his name?"

"Because Suriel said Harry saw him die?" Harry was puzzled too. He tried to think back to that night, to the moment Big Cass's bones and blood, skin and soul, had been scattered through the foliage of the riverbank.

"How did he die?" she asked, confirming that no, no she hadn't known this.

"Suriel killed him. Emma, how could you not—"

"Suriel can't kill a man—he's an angel!" she half laughed. "He's an angel bound to God—"

"Well, he did. I don't know what price he paid to do it, but he… blew the man up. His matter was all over the clearing—Suriel said Harry saw it too."

"Oh Lord," she breathed, standing up. "Yes. You're right, my darling. We have to make them be human."

Harry was so surprised—and so betrayed—he almost mreowled.

"Why?" Leonard sounded suspicious. "What are you thinking?"

"It's their fear. Suriel's unmaking of the man can only stay permanent if the boys believe he's gone. If they fear him every night…. Leonard, he's *real* to them. A magical end like that, it can be undone.

41

We need the boys to overcome their fears—and do it *now*—or that man will find his way back into their lives as sure as they're furry now and stalking mice!"

"Huh," Leonard said, sounding so puzzled, and dear Harry almost chuckled to himself.

"Why, whatever is wrong, dearest? You were in the right the whole time."

"Well, yes," Leonard admitted, "but this was not how I expected to win the argument. I almost wish it wasn't magical. I almost wish you'd just agreed with me because I love the boys as well."

Emma's voice softened. "Does it help that your affection for them only makes me fall deeper in love with you?" she asked sweetly.

"That is a fine consolation," he conceded.

What followed were kissing sounds—but fortunately by this time they had their own bedroom, and they made their way to it, leaving Harry awake in his corner, his heart threading in his throat as he contemplated the unthinkable.

Our fear could make him real.

He'd fought it then, had led the way for Edward and Francis, using their human form more often, for sitting at the table like men.

Anything, any amount of self-healing was worth it, as long as Big Cass would never be made flesh again.

As Harry blurred through the desert night, heading toward the encampment and hoping the men hunting their property couldn't move as fast as he did, he was praying as he hadn't prayed since he'd seen Suriel suffering.

Please let it not be him. Oh please. Let him be dead. Let him be gone. Let him not be about to kill my brothers and Suriel and the frightened women we stole from a terrible life. Oh please. Please. Please.

Please let Big Cass be dead.

By the time he got to the encampment, he'd been running full-out, front paws digging into the earth, back paws springing almost to his ears for the next bound, for nearly two miles. He started to slow down as he entered the light circle from the modest campfire—the one his brothers ranged around—but he was still going fast enough to be startled when he was plucked from the ground in midstride.

"Harry!" Edward hissed, shaking him. "Harry! What is going on inside your head? We couldn't hear you! Suriel was beside himself!"

Harry slid out of his grasp, taking shape as a human and gasping for breath. "Men… with guns…. *Big Cass!*"

That quickly, Francis and Suriel were there as humans, gathered around him.

"Harry, you're naked," Francis said calmly, and Harry glared at him while trying to pull in enough oxygen and coherent thought to make sense.

"Did you not hear what I said?" he asked, chest heaving. "Big Cass. I *saw* him. He was leading the others."

"That's impossible," Francis told him, an expression of serenity settling on his long features. "Big Cass is dead. Suriel blew him up. You told me that, and I believed you."

"It's true," Suriel said—but not as serenely. "I did blow him up. Harry, are you sure it was him?"

Harry nodded, but he couldn't meet Suriel's gaze. "We were so afraid," he said after a moment. "We were dreaming of him, years after it was over."

Edward grunted. "Yes."

"Emma said once… she said that our fear could bring him back to life. And I heard him talking—one of the men saw Suriel change into an eagle…." He *had* to look at Suriel now. "You were beautiful," he said softly, and Suriel's mouth parted on a smile. "But he started laughing and said that was the funniest thing he'd heard in a hundred years."

The silence thudded around them, creating a slow, viscous moment of settling fear.

"I… he's dead," Francis said with finality. "And he never touched me. I'm going to go check to make sure the deer are cooking well." He turned on his heel and stalked into the night.

"That's reassuring," Edward said dryly.

"And a lie," Harry said worriedly.

Edward grimaced. Harry had told him after that long-ago day, but not once had they heard Francis admit to either of them what had happened.

Now was not the time.

"I am nowhere *near* certain," Edward growled with a deep and cold hatred. "That bastard…." He and Harry looked at each other and shuddered. Harry had stood in front of Big Cass the first time he'd gone after Edward. He'd woken up with a head so sore he'd vomited for a week and a rip in his arse that hadn't quit bleeding for twice that long.

Before he could even walk again, Cass had taken Edward in front of him. He'd remember that moment, Edward, grim and silent, locking eyes with Harry and biting his lip as the two of them endured it together.

Yes. Edward could admit to the fear that had chased them through the ages.

"I saw him, Edward," Harry said quietly. "We need to keep him away from Francis—and the girls."

Edward's eyes filled with a profound sorrow. "And you, Harry. And me."

Harry gritted his teeth. "I'm not afraid. I'm not. I told you back then, remember?"

"Yes—and I believed you because I was young and stupid and I didn't see when someone was being brave for me so I didn't have to be brave for myself. You barely survived him, Harry. He hurt you worst of all." Edward shook his head and held out his hand to forestall any other conversation. "I'll go fetch you the last of the clothes." Suddenly he stopped and squinted as though his figures didn't add up. "Francis was right. How is it that both you and Suriel were naked when you changed?"

"We were, uh, washing the blood off," Harry muttered.

Edward cast him a suspicious glance and then stalked off toward the truck, where he'd probably stashed their emergency clothing satchel.

Leaving Suriel and Harry alone together on the edge of the light.

Suriel's hand on his shoulder sent warmth coursing down his adrenaline-cold body. "I'm sorry."

"For what?" Harry tried a smile. "Your plan was brilliant, and—" He bit his lip. "—it was a nice moment." Another flood of warmth that was all Harry's own coursed from his toes to his cheeks. Suriel brushed his cheekbone with a tender knuckle.

"I love this color in your face, on your body. Are you embarrassed or aroused, Harry?"

"Both," Harry said gruffly. Yeah, he'd been a whore once upon a time, but since then it was a rare man who got to see Harry naked— inside *or* out.

"Don't be embarrassed around me," Suriel said, voice sober. "Especially not about being frightened."

Harry swallowed hard. "I'm not frightened. He was a bogeyman from my childhood—"

"He was a terrible man, and he did terrible things to my boys." Suriel's bearing, which had been quizzical and curious since Harry had awakened in his arms, changed, so smoothly Harry could almost forget his delight at the watering hole. "I will not allow him to harm you or the others again."

Oh. "I'm grown." Harry tried to sound dignified. "If their fear conjured him up, then I'll protect them."

Suriel's sorrow hit him like a hammer blow. "You are so sure it was *their* fear, Harry?"

He had nowhere to go. The circles of women were off-limits—a naked man was the thing they all hated and feared the most. His brothers wouldn't believe him, and they certainly wouldn't sympathize, not if he'd called this thing down upon their heads.

"I conquered this fear," he said staunchly. "The others could scarcely turn human, and I ate dinner with Emma and Leonard *every night for a year*. I made them be human for our lessons. I learned hand-to-hand and weapons training so I could show them and we could fight. I *fought* this fear. I'm not the one who—"

Suriel's fingers on his chin were so soft Harry couldn't even jerk his head to turn away. "You're so very brave, my black heart, but fighting a fear every day of your life doesn't mean you've defeated it.

It just means you build a shell around yourself so you don't let any comfort in."

Harry's mouth fell open, and at that moment Edward approached with the clothes. He paused a moment to look at the two of them—Suriel wearing borrowed shorts with the belt taken way in, which meant they must have been Harry's, as well as a T-shirt—and Harry standing nude and working hard not to be self-conscious.

"Swimming. Harry, seriously, didn't you tell him you could have jumped in as cats and it all would have washed up when you were…." Edward took them in, standing intimately close together, Suriel with his fingers on Harry's chin. "Oh."

"He's the smart one," Harry said viciously, grabbing the clothes out of his hands.

"I'm smart enough to know why this didn't happen a hundred years ago!" Edward snapped back. "And it has nothing to do with Suriel not wanting it!"

Harry dropped the last set of clothes in the dirt with a distracted curse and picked them up while muttering to himself. Edward crouched in the dirt next to him and handed him a folded pair of socks with a courteous flip of his hand.

"We need to go out on patrol," Harry said. "I'm probably about twenty minutes ahead—"

"Did they know which direction? Suriel said he flew in a big circle."

Harry closed his eyes and thought. "You're right—but the campfires—"

"Mullins gave me a shielding spell," Edward said blithely.

"I thought he wasn't allowed to help us either!" Twenty years earlier, Mullins had stopped being called into their circle. Like Suriel, the cause had something to do with the conditions upon which he'd been allowed to join in the first place, but Edward had seemed angry about it, and they were scrupulous about not intruding. Too much time in each other's heads, sleeping in piles of fur and muscle, being part of a hardworking team and family unit. Hell, they'd seen each other having sex plenty of times in the brothel. Staying out of each other's business felt like they'd given each other their humanity back.

Harry wouldn't ask about Mullins any more than Edward had asked about Suriel—until, apparently, they showed up naked together after a hunt.

"Well, he risked a hell of a lot to sneak into our campfire and give me this spell," Edward said grimly. "Something must be up. So yeah, we'll set patrols—but you have to promise to stay online and in our heads. Francis was freaking the hell out!"

Harry struggled for something to say. "I was rattled" came out at the last.

"I was there," Edward growled. "Do you think I don't know? Do you think you're fooling anyone but yourself?"

Harry stood and handed him everything but the boxers, then slid those on first. "Can we not talk about this—"

"Sure, Harry, 'cause this has been festering like a boil in your soul for a hundred and forty years. Why would we want to talk about it *now* when it's about ready to erupt in our faces!"

Edward was best at it, but they'd both trained in medicine for a number of years, and now they paused. "Ew," Harry said.

"Yeah, sorry about that. Gross. But do you see my point here?"

A man's voice, shouting an order, carried clearly through the night, and both of them stiffened and listened. "You take south, Francis takes east, and I'll head straight down the middle. They can't see me at night." Harry had always been the best at strategy and the first to command.

"What shall I do?" Suriel asked, and Harry looked at him, miserable. How long did he have? How long did *they* have, to finish all the things they needed to say to one another before Suriel would go back to heaven forever and Harry would be stuck down on earth, as alone in his heart as he'd always been?

"Is the truck running?"

Suriel thought hard, and all three of them grimaced as the sound of grinding metal told them about instantaneous truck repair. "Sure."

"Okay—gather the girls and the food and load them in it. Can you drive that thing?"

"Sure, Harry, if you're behind the wheel operating the gears and controls."

Harry stared, and Edward held back a snicker. "You heard him, Harry—he's going nowhere without you. Gather everyone up, Suriel, and we'll figure out how badly we're screwed."

Harry yanked his clothes on, glaring at Suriel the whole time. "You could have just said no," he muttered as Edward turned cat and began to broadcast the plan to Francis.

"But then you might have run off into the night and gotten killed without me." Suriel was all practicality. "I'd really rather be by your side."

Harry finished with his clothes, uncertain of what to say.

Finally, only the truth would do.

"I wouldn't mind that last thing," he said wretchedly, and then he changed and darted back out into the night.

FRANCIS'S PALE fur should have glowed like the moon, attracting attention of man and beast as they all slid through the night, but something about Francis just didn't allow that to happen. Instead, he was a patch of moonlight on the desert sand, the absence of a snake, the brighter shadow of a darker patch of tumbleweed.

Harry, smoky, furry black, was hardly a whisper as he found his way from shadow to shadow, like stepping stones across a pool.

No—Harry and Francis had always excelled at camouflage. It was Edward who couldn't hide a piece of risotto in a rice bin.

That's why Edward always hung back in the rear, so if they were doing recon and things went to shit, he could find a way to bail everybody's ass out of the fire.

In this case, it saved their lives.

The three domestic house cats flitted from the flickering borders of the campfire circles to the shadows beyond. Harry looked behind him and—now that he knew it was there—could see Mullins's dampening spell, fooling the unwary eye into just seeing more desert. He blinked once, and the women—refreshed now with some rest, some cooked deer, some water—were moving back into the truck with what looked to be hope.

Suriel, still bright and shining, a beacon of angelic light against the darkness, raised his hand and waved, as though he could see Harry as he skittered through the brush. Harry flicked his whiskers and then his tail in that direction, just in case he could.

Then Harry was all business, running point, directing the other two back in the direction from which danger threatened.

The click of ammunition and thump of combat boots alerted them first. All three of them found cover—in Harry's case, another creosote bush—and ducked behind it to listen for information.

"The truck was definitely heading north," someone said. Harry thought it might have been the same man, small, wiry, and hunched, who had actually acknowledged that Suriel was an eagle.

"Doesn't mean it'll keep going that way in the desert." This speaker, slightly taller, with a scraggly beard and missing teeth, fidgeted while he spoke, poking the shadows with his toes, tapping the brush with the end of his gun. "Hard to go in a straight line in the desert."

A few others gathered with them, same five or so folks Harry had seen the first time, and like the first time, the next speaker set up an ice storm in Harry's bowels.

"Yeah, but these boys—they've got a goal. You don't steal a truckload of cattle without having a place to sell them or set them to graze free-range. They've got a plan."

A bright red ball of hatred pushed against Harry's brain, and he and Edward were suddenly all soothing blue. *Francis, calm down. Chill, little brother—find your peace.*

Cattle!

Bad guys!

Kill… kill kill kill….

Not yet!

Francis was fully capable of killing the soulless where they stood, but quick as he was, he would only take down one or two of them before their wicked-looking semiautomatics would gut him so badly not even Suriel could fix him. Bad guys didn't often talk—which was, perhaps, why Francis had lived so long.

They had calmed Francis down into a not-quite-feral, hissing ball of hatred when Harry spotted the hulking shadow of his nightmares.

49

His breath caught in his throat, and his claws chewed at the earth.

But he must not, *must not* become Francis.

Do you see that? he demanded from Edward.

Right now I see your tail starting a sandstorm. Shut up for a second and let me listen.

"They went east," Big Cass snarled. "I can smell their campfires. Now hurry, and let's take 'em out before they get away with the damned cows that started this mess, yeah?"

Big Cass's speech cadences were off—his accent spoke of a hundred years ago, on the dirty cobblestone streets next to a river that flooded every year.

Why doesn't he speak modern? Harry asked, mostly to derail the seething ball of hate and rage that Francis was becoming.

I don't give a shi—

We study, Harry, Edward said didactically. *We immerse ourselves in this world for art and history and good. He just wants to know when his next shipment is coming in. We have bigger minds.*

Francis, Harry added for good measure.

The seething went from danger red to cold and icy white, and Harry started to outline a plan.

It depended on the three of them and their gifts.

Francis was good with the confusion spell, and Edward was stealthy and good with fire spells. Harry was best with the frontal attack, and the one most practiced at killing when they needed to.

Harry could also turn from cat to human and back again so smoothly and so quickly, people frequently doubted they had seen a cat *or* a man.

We need to lure them into the desert, he began, *but we don't have much time. If we can get them lost, take one or two of them out—*

Edward's mental voice, sharp and panicked, jumped into their strategy meeting. *There's someone coming from this way!*

"Did you find them?"

Harry left off his preoccupation with Big Cass for a more immediate fear.

"I can smell 'em," Cass muttered. "But these clowns claim they can't see nothin'."

"You'd best listen to him, boys. He's got the gift of smelling out escapees, you hear? It's downright uncanny."

Harry turned his head and saw a big man, bigger than Cass, older in appearance by a decade, but with a body fit and hard as granite.

"Aw, sweetheart." Cass turned his head and spat. "You're talkin' so pretty I might have to blow you right here."

"You'll bend over and take it," the newcomer snarled, and Cass gave him a look of desire and disgust that told Harry that yes—that was exactly the relationship the two of them had.

Harry's fear lessened at the same time his hatred increased. These two men were all that Harry and his brothers had fought so hard to overcome in their long, long lifetime—they knew what pain, what poison they spread, and they did it anyway, for the joy of destruction.

"Yeah, sure, Oldham," Cass spat, a cruel twist to his mouth. "I'll take it—but first we gotsta get the cattle back. I'm not bendin' over in the fuckin' desert—too much sand."

Oldham laughed. "Right—so which way did the bitches go?"

"East—I smell diesel that way, and a campfire and deer." From Harry's vantage point, he watched as Big Cass's nose twitched, almost like a cat's but missing that last bit of shifting ability that would have made it a solid part of his identity. "I smell cats too—smelled 'em the last time we lost a shipment, in Vegas. Thought it was an accident, but there's somethin' here."

Oldham's black eyebrows went up, striking in his otherwise pale face and bald pate. "Cats, like, pussycats?"

Big Cass bared his teeth. "Cats, like predators. Cats. I'm tellin' ya, I smelled cat piss like this before—maybe they sell cats for coats, but it's the same outfit."

Oldham grunted. "You're the only one that survived, Cass. I'm not gonna doubt you, but I don't know what to do with the smell of cat piss and roast deer."

Unexpectedly Cass burst out into raucous laughter. "Just follow me, gents. I got a whiff of something ripe and crispy."

Francis, please tell me that's you, Edward begged.

51

Francis's response was unamused, and Harry twitched his tail in a cat version of a snicker.

C'mon, Edward—he doesn't smell that bad.

Francis's response was a silent feline hiss.

Seriously, Francis, Harry asked as the men started to move out. *Is that your doing or should we try to stop them?*

It's me. I sent them southeast instead of northeast. But we've got to get out of here or he'll smell us for real.

Freaky, that, Edward said, voicing it for all of them.

Harry grunted and took off toward the hunting party, thinking hard about the various weapons he'd seen as the men had gathered. He was particularly good at a spell that could make a gun fire without warning— but he needed to see it aimed in the right direction to provoke a fiasco like they'd caused in Colorado. It was only something one wanted to do with lots of empty land for miles around. The people they were up against were often not bright, nor were they particularly good shots, but it was best if Harry and his brothers were at maximum safe distance, and hopefully out of sight.

"Hey, where you assholes going?"

Bless me and sneeze, Harry—we've got a minion-come-lately.

"And where did the damned cats— Ouch! What in the fu—"

Jesus, Francis—we've got to help him!

Edward, who was usually their most solid thinker, had neglected to turn human and literally leaped up into the latecomer's face and was fighting like a warrior—or a twenty-pound tomcat who thought he could fly.

Harry had to turn his back on Big Cass, Oldham, and the others and trust that they'd keep running into the desert as Francis had led them, following the imaginary smell of cat pee and burned deer. For the moment, his brother needed him.

Edward's victim was trying to wrestle Edward like a man would wrestle a man, not a cat. Edward, Harry, and Francis had once brought down a wild boar when food was scarce. He knew how to dig in with his sharpened claws and rip at vulnerable places—the enemy's eyes, his neck, his throat. The blood poured copiously, the spill of it made worse by Edward's knowledge of medicine and some *very* dark magics that Mullins had no business teaching anybody, but Edward just suddenly knew one year after they'd all sustained some nasty wounds.

In the long term, the man would probably die, but he was desperate enough to start sweeping his locked semiauto along his back, and Edward got knocked off with a shrill howl of pain.

The man had time to pivot and aim before Harry leaped at him, turning human as he did. He knocked the gun out of the villain's hand, and broke his jaw with one well-timed blow of his elbow.

The late-coming henchman staggered back, moaning and shouting, and Harry turned and kicked out precisely, dislocating his knee. He went down, and Harry took out his gonads with enough force to rupture and was going in to break his ribs and puncture his heart when Francis charged out of the night, leaped over the downed henchman, and disappeared in the direction they'd come from.

His mind radiated the distinct, acrid-smelling terror of Big Cass.

Now, Harry! Francis barked in his head, and Harry took off running, turning cat along the way and leaving the bleeding villain in the sand behind him. Hell—oh hell, hell, hell and damnation.

If the man lived, he'd talk about shapeshifting cats.

If he died, his corpse would tell a very peculiar tale of its own.

Francis! Harry called. *Francis—let us catch up. I'm using the fog spell, dammit—you need to be in my radius!*

Next to him, as Edward ran awkwardly, tucking his broken front leg against his chest, he felt the startlement and, yes, fear.

Harry hadn't exactly mastered this spell the last time he'd tried it.

But dammit, he could hear the men behind them stumbling in the dark, and the minute they spied their downed companion, bullets would be careening after the three feline specters who had wrought so much havoc.

Francis! Harry roared and was rewarded by the hint of a ghostly tail. Francis had slowed down just enough for them to run together, and that's all Harry needed.

Caligo pedibus felis parvae venit Caligo pedibus felis parvae venit Caligo pedibus felis parvae venit....

For spells, poetry was the best, and what was more arcane than Carl Sandburg?

Maybe it was the adrenaline boost from knowing Big Cass was behind them—maybe that's what did it. But as Harry wrote the incantation in his mind—using a fiery brand against black, which seemed to work best for him—and the fog rolled in, churning, thick, and nearly sentient, it wasn't fear in his heart. It was the idea of Suriel, sitting patient and stubborn in the uncomfortable vinyl seat of the semitruck.

As mist overtook Harry and his brothers, their forms became insubstantial, and then they *became* the fog, rolling away from the violence and the anger at their backs.

This is great, Francis said, sudden tranquility tinging his thoughts a light gray. *What happens if they get lost in us?*

I have no idea. For a moment, Harry almost broke concentration. His body flashed into solidity and then out again as his cat and the fog became interchangeable. He felt Francis and Edward's panic in his mind, and a stark terror of having his molecules flung indiscriminately about the desert almost destroyed them all.

And then he thought of Suriel again, of his kiss under the open sky.

About how he'd wanted to kiss Harry for ages.

Peace assailed him, and his fiery center burned bright. The spell became real again, and he and his brothers were themselves at their cores, although their bodies drifted in the fog of his making.

They rolled swiftly, carried on no wind of this earth, until Harry spotted the truck sitting unlit and alone, a few feet from the road it had been traveling as Harry passed out.

With a conscious effort, Harry released the spell, and the three of them kept running as cats. The smell of clean-burning diesel almost overwhelmed him, after the moments of having no lungs at all, but he was still relieved.

Warmed up and ready. Suriel must have been paying attention to know the truck wouldn't just start on a dime.

Francis and I will take the back, Edward said before smoothly morphing into a human, broken limb realigned by shapeshifting—and perhaps even fog. Francis stayed cat; they had learned in previous missions that very often a serene, furry, seemingly helpless companion could calm and bond frightened people. Francis—angelic, blue-eyed Francis—could be credited for stopping fear riots with just a few strategic meows.

The screech of the roll-door ripped through the night as Edward let himself and Francis in, while Harry jogged toward the front. Of the three of them, he was the only one who had a class three license—and the only one who really enjoyed the big rig.

He swung up into the front seat and grinned in the face of Suriel's sober-eyed attention. "Thanks for warming her up for me!"

"You have blood on your shirt," Suriel said severely. Harry looked down as he secured his belt and disengaged both sets of brakes.

"Only some of it was mine," he soothed. "And it all went away with the changes."

Not all wounds could be cured by changing forms—the one Harry had suffered before Suriel had arrived could very possibly have killed him. But all he'd done with the henchman was bloody his knuckles and sustain a crack across the jaw with an elbow.

Suriel rubbed his jawbone with a careful thumb. "It was dislocated until you changed," he said, and although his voice was pitched above the engine noise, it rumbled low in Harry's stomach.

Harry caught his hand. Following an impulse he'd never before acknowledged, he kissed Suriel's perfect knuckles.

"Please don't worry, my pretty angel," he said whimsically. "It will be glory in the morning." And with that he let go of Suriel's hand, shifted hard, and put the thing into gear. The truck rolled smoothly to the edge of the road, and after a triple-check with headlights to make sure he had at least a half mile to accelerate, he released the brake again and stepped on the gas.

The great metal beast growled ferociously and rumbled on a smooth course onto the road—toward the freeway again, so Harry could make the stop.

"Where are you taking them?" Suriel asked after a few moments.

"Visalia," Harry answered promptly. "Emma's contacts will meet us there—a fleet of minivans, usually. Moms with clothes to fit teenage girls. The vans split up, the girls go to safe houses and either get sent back to their own families or assimilated into this country. None of it's aboveboard, and most of it is downright illegal." He finished that last with a cheeky wink. As the Youngblood family had progressed into their third century, they'd become increasingly contemptuous of the bureaucracy that seemed to get in the way of much that was human compassion. They were as much outlaws as they were freedom fighters, and Leonard got a tremendous amount of satisfaction hacking government systems to sweep away the damage path some of their missions left behind.

He said computerized misinformation was the most powerful magic he'd ever wielded.

"You take a great deal of pleasure from violating the rules." The frown line between Suriel's light brown eyebrows managed to make him look both grave *and* precious. Harry wasn't sure how he did that. Maybe it was four millennia of consciousness, or maybe it was having a damned fine taste in bodies.

"We do," Harry said proudly, pulling his mind back to the road and the conversation. "Is that a problem?"

"No," Suriel mused. "It's just, all these years, and I expected you to fall in love with Mullins."

Harry took a big breath and steadied his hands on the rig. "That's… odd."

Harry, are you okay? Are they following us? Your brain sounds… numb.

Harry checked the mirrors quickly. He was nearing I-5, in the wee hours of the morning. There weren't many cars on the road, so the headlights in his rearview might mean trouble.

But not yet.

Suriel just said something surprising, he told Edward. *It's not important.*

"Are you telling Edward?" Suriel asked, voice mild.

"No. Because brother or not, magical binding or not, he would shank me in my fuckin' sleep."

Suriel's laughter burbled up over the engine noise. "He would not."

Harry rolled his eyes. "Perhaps—but I wouldn't be too sure. Edward's been sweet on Mullins since…." Oh hell. "Since that first night. I wouldn't, in a million years, try to get between the two of them."

"What if Edward had been 'sweet' on me?" Suriel asked gently.

Harry tried to contain his despair. "I wouldn't have gotten in his way," he rasped. "You… you understand, we'd do anything to see each other happy. If I even *knew* what Francis wanted half the time, I'd run through broken glass to fetch it." But Francis… darling Francis only ever seemed to want to be held as a cat, or to nap in a sunspot—or Bel's lap. From the moment that child was born, Francis had elected himself lone baby protector. Harry and Edward were capable of second-rate jobs at best.

"That's very noble, Harry," Suriel said, but he didn't sound happy about it. "What about what you want for yourself?"

Harry let out a grunt. "I've only wanted a handful of things in my life," he said, accelerating the truck so it could make the overpass. For a moment the silence threatened to take over, and then Suriel lost his temper.

"Harry, I'm here on earth for what may be the last time. Please, for the love of heaven, don't make me wait for an answer."

Harry found a smile inside his ever-fighting heart. "Suriel, I've never heard you get pissed before. That was amazing—care to do it again?"

"*Dammit, Harry!*"

The truck lifted a good six inches into the air and clunked down again, and Harry fought to keep it on the road as he rounded the on-ramp.

"God*dammit*, Suriel!"

"Answer me! Your heart has been wounded, leaking hope like a sieve, for *years*. Your family has felt it, Harry—they've begged me to help, and I couldn't, because helping you would break my binding with God. And now here I am, ready to tip into mortality, to break my binding anyway. The least you could do is say it. Open your mouth and tell me the thing you want that you're so afraid to reach for. You're so brave, Harry! You lead your brothers into every fight, and you are fearless. You face death and you are unafraid—"

"I'm unafraid because I know you'll be waiting!" Harry cried, not wanting Suriel to be fooled. "Because if you can't save me in this life, I know you'll be waiting in the next. *That's* why I'm unafraid. Because I know that if I die, you'll be there, in heaven, and for once you won't have to leave when the candle gutters and the rooster crows. Are you happy now? Is that what you wanted to hear? That it's not a death wish, no matter *how* fucking lonely I am. It's a *you* wish—how's that?"

The car in front of them was suddenly *too* close. Harry checked to his left and yanked on the wheel as hard as he dared. The semi swerved out into the passing lane, and Harry checked his mirror and saw a car speeding up, like it was *trying* to rear-end them.

"Dammit. They're trying to swoop and squat—"

"They're flying?" Suriel asked, that puzzled, curious part of him coming into play again.

"No—it's an old conman's game—try to get the sucker to hit you so you'll stop and give them insurance money. In this case they're trying to get me to hit them because they want me to stop, period."

Suriel grunted. "Are these the same people you chased in the desert?"

Harry took a look in his rearview and tried to make out the features of the guy driving the red pickup truck he'd almost passed.

His stomach was never going to stop freezing when he saw Big Cass. "Yup," he muttered, accelerating. Even as he did, he watched as the red truck with Big Cass and the gray one that almost hit them both picked up speed as well. "They're not giving up." He hated this thought, but it was probably true. "I bet we killed the guy Edward attacked. Mullins showed him all sorts of black-magic moves to open up his throat—those worked pretty well."

"I am not excited about that direction in Edward's magic," Suriel said primly. "If *Edward* dies, it would be wonderful if he was heading to heaven as well."

"Do you think Mullins would let him go anywhere else?" Harry asked—and not sarcastically.

"So you know Mullins loves Edward but you won't even hazard a guess about me?" Suriel demanded.

"A missed guess with you would destroy me," Harry answered, distracted enough by the chase that the rawness of this conversation, the risks he was taking making himself vulnerable, weren't tying his tongue into the usual knots. "I'm only brave with my life, Suriel, not my heart. *Down, dammit!*"

They drew near again, and this time Harry saw the headlight gleam on the ugly black butt of an automatic weapon.

Harry checked his rearview, saw that the only vehicle right behind him was the other truck.

Great. They wanted a conman's car accident? Harry would give one to them, Youngblood style! He sped up, heedless of Francis and Edward swearing up a storm in his head, and used the momentum and power of the relatively empty semi to pull even with the big Ford pickup. "I said get down!" he snarled to Suriel, and when Suriel had complied, lying full-length across the seat, his head touching Harry's thigh, Harry pulled the horn.

Big Cass looked right at him, and Harry's night vision was just as good as a man as it was when he was feline. Harry saw Cass's eyes widen and his mouth fall open, before he pulled his lips back in a sneer and hit his brakes.

Harry shot ahead, and the semi juddered hard as Cass rammed the side with the truck. Ridiculous in one way because Harry could flatten him, but in another way—

Cass hit again, and Edward and Francis both screamed in his head. The girls were in danger, and Harry needed to do something.

Harry changed lanes, the metal of the Ford grinding against the side of the truck before it broke free, and the entire human collective inside gave a big gasp of relief. In the rearview, Harry saw the F-150 go tumbling into the desert and the blue Chevy slowing down to follow it off-road—without the tumble.

Everyone okay back there?

A couple of the girls got hurt. I'm tending to them. Francis was upset enough to change form, and now they're all plastered on the cab end of the cargo bay. Edward's slightly dry mental voice broke into a wholly inappropriate cackle. *He's trying to speak Russian and Spanish simultaneously. It sounds like he's speaking Martian, and it's scaring them more.*

Oh jeez—it wasn't funny in the least. The girls were terrified, and Big Cass had almost taken more victims than just Harry, Edward, and Francis. It should have been the most serious thing in the world but....

But there were no serious injuries, and Harry had faith in his brothers.

He chortled out loud, startling Suriel into sitting up. Harry's thigh went cold without the spill of red-gold hair over it, but he kept his eyes on the road.

"What's so funny?"

"Francis flipped out and went human in the back. He's trying to speak to the girls in two languages at once, and they think he's from outer space." Harry broke up again, gleeful as he hadn't been in... well, a year.

Since the last time Suriel had come to talk to them, from midnight until morning.

Suriel laughed politely, and Harry sobered.

"It was him," he said after a minute. "I'd like to think he was killed when his truck endoed, but not this guy. He's a cockroach, apparently. Survive anything."

"That depends." Suriel looked into his rearview mirror incuriously. The two trucks were long gone from sight anyway.

"On what?"

"Are you still afraid of him?"

Harry took a deep breath and prepared to say "Hell no!"

Suriel wrapped a possessive hand around his thigh, and he let that breath right out again.

"What do you want me to say?" If he was speaking to a human man, his voice would be too low to hear over the engine noise. But he wasn't speaking to a human man.

"I want you to talk to me about him, Harry. Tell me why he scares the three of you so much."

Harry grunted. "Didn't figure you for a voyeur." He prayed Suriel would move his hand, but he only squeezed a little harder.

"You'd be surprised about that—but this isn't voyeurism. Yes, I know he raped you and the others. Is that what you wanted me to say? We all know that—all the people in your life know this is a fact, Harry. But you know something? I know this for a fact because I asked. These last five years, you throwing yourself into every damned fray headfirst, you're damned right I asked. You have never, not once, said it. Edward told Mullins, back during World War I. Francis told Emma—"

"Sometime in the first couple years," Harry said gruffly. "I know. We didn't know about Francis then. We thought—the whole reason we were in that clearing was me and Edward trying to get him out before... before it happened."

"You didn't think Big Cass would get him before that? He's a very handsome boy."

Harry half laughed. "You should have seen him when he was a baby—his voice had hardly dropped. Before I saw you, I thought he looked like an angel. Edward too. Too pretty to be in that place."

Suriel sighed and fiddled with the switches on the dashboard. Cool air blew in, and Harry half smiled. He'd forgotten temperature controls in all the excitement. Then Suriel fiddled some more, and a country-western station played. Harry rather liked country-western—he smiled all the way, pleased.

"You were all beautiful boys," Suriel said into the softened silence. "I saw you."

Harry shrugged. "I was plain. Cass, Bertha—they said it often enough. Said I wouldn't make it as a whore—too plain, too mouthy." He smiled grimly. "The 'mouthy' wasn't really a problem in that business, it turned out."

Suriel flicked him on the temple—hard.

"Goddamn—"

"Unnecessary," Suriel growled. "And crude. No joking about those days—not tonight. Not when death keeps trying to run you down and your fear keeps letting it."

The vastness of I-5 ran steadily under the big rig's wheels, and the sky opened up so clear, with so many stars and a stately silver moon, Harry could have seen the road ahead without headlights. With headlights, the battered asphalt looked haunted and infinite, and the dry waste of what should have been ripe farmland roared on either side of the highway like a lifeless ocean.

Harry thought hard, tried to summon up what Big Cass had been to him as a child. Tried to encapsulate the fear, the bone-grinding, gawdawful fear that had chewed at the three of them, every minute of every day, from the moment they'd entered the brothel in the care of their mothers to the moment they'd escaped, running for their lives.

PLAINLY

"ME MUM——" He swallowed and remembered—this was twenty-first-century California. The years hadn't passed Harry's family in a vacuum, and neither had the speech patterns. "My mother's family was pretty well off, back east. My father wanted to earn his fortune, I guess. They came to California after the war—the Civil War. My father fought for the North. They were sort of the second wave, the merchant wave, wanting to make a living here, when back in Boston it felt like all of the merchants had been there since the revolution. They settled in Hangtown—Placerville—and she had three babies, boom, boom, boom. He got a job for the railroad as foreman and died when they were gouging a trench in the Sierras to drive a bloody great train through."

He had to take a cleansing breath, trying to rid himself of some of the anger he'd had back then—but Suriel wouldn't let him keep even his anger.

"Why does that irritate you?"

Harry grunted. "The railroad—sheer hubris. There arc ways to live in the world without ripping a hole in it."

"But people didn't think that way back then. You can't hold it against your father that he was trying to feed his family."

"I can hold it against him that he died," Harry snapped. "He died and left my mother with a pittance for a pension. None of her family would help her because he'd been such an irritating bastard before he left, telling them all that he could do it by himself, take care of her and such. She traveled down to Sacramento to sell her things—hcr rich dresses, some furniture—but thieves beset us on the way there." Harry remembered that night; he'd been no more than nine, his sisters even younger. She'd hidden them in the woods by the wagon while the two men had unloaded all the things they'd owned, and thcn—oh, Harry had watched from the shadows as they'd bent his mother over and taken the last thing she had left.

By the time she got to Sacramento, sick and sore, a few months in the brothel were all she had in her. It was enough to save money for two tickets. She sent Harry to buy them, because she hadn't trusted Bertha, not even at death's door. He'd come back, and she'd had him take his sisters, with tiny cloth bags filled with a change of clothes and letters to their grandmother.

He remembered, clear as day, Laura and Molly waving to him from a train window, looking hurt and vulnerable and young. Was the last time he'd seen them—and he couldn't think of them now as dead, both of them, after a good long life surrounded by children.

"I'm sorry, Harry," his mother rasped when he'd returned from the station. Her body shuddered, wracked with fever and dying. "You're such a good protector, my brave boy. I can only hope God protects you here."

He swallowed against the memory. "My mother got to Sacramento, made enough to send my sisters away, and then died in the brothel. Bertha said I could work off the rest of her debts." He laughed humorlessly. "I wasn't more than nine or ten. Took me a year or two to realize there were worse things than cleaning toilets."

Suriel grunted. "That still makes you only twelve. Edward was fourteen when they started looking at him to work—so was Francis."

Harry grinned, feral and vicious. "Well, I learned some tricks to keep Big Cass and the customers away from them, oh yes I did." Oh, his accent. He shook his head. "I figured out," he tried again, "that if I used my mouth on Big Cass—voluntarily—I could give Edward time to get away. Then...." Oh Lord. "One day he got Edward. I tried...." His voice broke. "I tried to stop him, but... I'm sure Edward told you about that."

"Edward said you almost died."

"He shouldn't have even been there," Harry said, body flushing with the injustice. "His mother didn't even whore for Bertha. She was looking for an inn! And she had Edward with her, and she got sick—" Harry swore, the anger surprising him. "I always thought Bertha must have drugged her and overdid it. And Edward—he was young too.

Younger than me, but… but he shouldn't have been there. And I tried to protect him, but—"

"But you were a child, and you failed." Suriel's voice was a mercy.

"Yes."

"Why the fear? This is your past, and—" Harry glanced at him, because it wasn't like Suriel to let his voice break. "It's hurting me in ways I didn't know I could be hurt." Suriel was staring out the front window, biting his lip. Harry reached out and clasped his hand briefly, wondering that he was so soft, so far gone in the matter of Suriel, that he would volunteer that much affection without being prompted. But Suriel brought Harry's knuckles to his lips, much like Harry had done earlier that long night, and kissed them. "You were brave then—I knew it that night when I picked you up. Why so afraid of Big Cass? Help me understand. He could have been shattered out there in the desert, Harry. Gutted, destroyed—but your fear—I can feel it, pouring into the night. It will resurrect him and heal him, as sure as we're both stuck here, when there are so many other things I would do with you during my time on earth."

Harry's chest hurt. "How much time do you have here?"

"We were talking about—"

"*Please*, Suriel. Please tell me how much time you have." His mind was trapped in the past, and his body was trapped on this mission. How long did he have to free them both so he could look Suriel in the eye and tell him the things he'd been afraid to say for so very long?

"It depends on how much power I'm forced to use," Suriel said softly. "I should get a sevenday from the time I became corporeal, and then I'll have to choose."

Harry tried to think. "So, late afternoon yesterday—we have six and a half days?"

"Unless I have to pull you back from death again," Suriel said grimly.

"I'll try not to let that happen." Harry's voice held all the sincerity in the world. Quiet again, Harry saw lights in his rearview, and he sighed, accelerating just a touch. They had a hundred miles to go—it wasn't much. If they could just get to the vacant school in Visalia without incident, the boys could see the girls to safety, and Harry and Suriel... they could talk.

Harry could see what Suriel wanted from him, could learn all he could give to help Suriel go back to heaven without being punished, without suffering for the bindings of his heart to Harry, when his soul and service had been bound already.

But first....

"Please, my brave boy." Suriel's voice throbbed painfully at the endearment—and for the first time, Harry recognized how much being Suriel's "brave boy" meant to him.

"Suriel—"

"Please, tell me why the fear. He was a bully and a rapist—and those are dreadful things. But you have overcome so much worse, and it has been so long. What is this terror that looms so greatly in your heart?"

"I wish I was anywhere but here," Harry whispered wretchedly, keeping his eyes on the road.

"Alone?" The hurt was unmistakable.

"No. With you. You kissed me, Suriel—why did you do that?"

"I've longed to for over a century," Suriel confessed. "You're avoiding the—"

"No. No, I'm not." Harry pulled his fingers through his hair. Over the years he'd tried a variety of styles, but unlike Edward who liked his cut short and conventional to the times, Harry always liked his a bit long. He thought back to that kiss, him and Suriel, and wondered what it would feel like to have Suriel's fingers pulling through it until it was soft.

He took a deep breath and tried to put it into words.

"I was all alone there before Edward came," he said at last. "My mother died, Edward's hadn't arrived yet—and I was alone. And I kept hearing my mother's words, hoping God would protect me, and I was so dumb, you know? A kid. I tried to dodge Big Cass, and I made sure I was covered in shit whenever he was near. I was kind to all the girls—they protected me as much as they could. But when it finally happened, right up until the...."

"Pain," Suriel said gruffly.

"Yeah. Right up until that moment, I thought God would protect me. And then the pain hit, and there was this bright gold light behind my eyes, and I thought... thought he had."

"Oh. Oh, Harry."

Harry tried to keep his voice steady, and definitely tried to keep his eyes clear. "But then, then I realized what the light was, and that... that Big Cass had... and I know the difference now. I get it. I get that the hand of the divine can't be everywhere. It's got to be in the hearts of the protectors—that's the only way good belays the executioner's axe. But back then I was alone, and I was violated, and Big Cass was my god. And he was a god with a black heart, and the despair...."

"You aren't alone anymore."

Harry laughed. "Emma's been saying that for nearly a century and a half, Suriel. And the only time I ever felt it—felt it in my furry bones— was when I was with you."

Suriel's hand on his knee was not a surprise. But the way it spread warmth through his body, to his groin, to his chest—that was new.

Harry, how long do we have? Edward's voice intruded on the moment and the desire. He and Edward—meticulous about being brothers to each other. Brothers in their hearts.

Two hours. I think all the trouble has passed us by. How are they doing?

Francis stopped trying to talk to them, turned back into a cat, and is now sulking in a corner. A few of the braver ones are gathered around him and trying to soothe his feelings.

Harry's chuckle echoed in the cab as well as in Edward's head.

He really does land on his feet, you know.

Every time. It's uncanny.

Harry started to pull away when Edward spoke again.

You... you feel sad. And fragile, my brother. Are you okay?

Suriel is asking me that same question. Why didn't you tell me you'd gone to him for help?

Because you were grieving without him. There was nothing any of us could do.

Next time, say something.

Why? So you could kill yourself proving you were fine? No, thank you. Unacceptable losses. Our family of eight—those losses are unacceptable. We decided that a long time ago, remember, brother?

Oh hells. *Why does every conversation with you mean I have to bare my soul to someone else?* he demanded uncharitably.

Edward's almost evil chuckle did not reassure him.

Because you, me, and Francis are a disturbance of the natural order of things, Harry. Don't ever doubt it. Oh, hey—one of them has him on his back and is petting his stomach. His head's gone all slack and he's drooling. Damn—where's a camera phone when you need one?

Edward withdrew, but not before leaving Harry with a very undignified image of their little brother in a *very* undignified position. Harry touched on Francis's thoughts for a moment and only caught a pleasant, drugged haze, and then he was all himself again on the cheap vinyl of the big-rig cab.

"There's a bed in the back of this," Suriel said. As Harry had been preoccupied, he'd scooted closer until their shoulders, hips, and thighs were touching.

Harry had to pull his thoughts from the pure physicality of having Suriel's touch all to himself in private before he could address what Suriel was saying.

"Yeah—we've used the truck before, but we've never slept in it."

Suriel leaned closer to him to get a look at the snug little cabin in back. A mattress, clean sheets, pillows, even some books and a light set into the cab of the truck near the head of the bed—all the trappings of home.

"That's a shame," he said softly. "It looks cozy."

Harry shrugged—it had never impressed him. "Usually, if we have to stop and rest, one of us sleeps in back with the girls and the other two stay awake. We take turns. It doesn't feel right, one of us sleeping up here and the others vigilant. It's more right we're all together."

Suriel hummed—there was no other word for it.

"Thank you," he said just as he ran fingertips along the tight ridge of Harry's shoulder. Harry kept his eyes on the road, but his skin danced at the barest whisper of Suriel's touch.

"For what?"

"Telling me why you were so afraid. Did you think I wouldn't understand?"

Harry let out a sharp bark of laughter. "I told you that man killed God for me, Suriel—you're an *angel*. How much do you think I wanted you to know?"

Suriel laid his head on Harry's shoulder, and Harry spent a bare fraction of a breath turning his head and smelling the fire-gold fragrance of Suriel's loose hair.

A yawn took over Suriel's body, and Harry had to laugh. Apparently parts of being human took him by surprise.

"*You* want to use the bed, don't you?" he asked kindly.

Suriel shook his head and settled down more comfortably. "This is fine," he said through another yawn. "I just... I want you to know. I know you're still afraid of Big Cass—of having no faith in the world again, of being all alone. But you rebuilt faith in your heart with the love of your brothers, your parents—on that alone. That took more courage than facing Big Cass ever could."

Suriel yawned again, and then, like a child, fell asleep.

Harry was left with the roar of the diesel engine and the hum of the tires on the tattered pavement as they rumbled through the night.

MORNINGS IN Mendocino were frequently cold. It didn't snow there often, but there was usually a sharp, wet wind blowing off the ocean, and the combination of cold and damp could chill a man to his vitals, make brittle his viscera and bones.

Within a week of moving to the tiny, drafty cabin that would become a mansion—and their home—Harry realized that Emma, who had power at her fingertips to command as an old and studied witch, woke up early every morning to start a fire in the Ben Franklin stove in the center of the room.

The boys had gotten used to sleeping as cats very quickly; they preferred it. Cats woke up fully, in an instant—nobody surprised a cat in the way Big Cass had been known to surprise the boys. And they were furry and, if they slept in a huddle, warm.

Always warm.

But Emma would get up early anyway, stoke the fire, and put on hot water for tea or coffee.

After a week, Harry was curious enough to turn human to ask her what she was doing.

First she greeted him with a warm sweater and thick socks to pull on, as well as a stocking cap and a blanket over his shoulders—the cold was stunning.

Then she poured him a hot cup of coffee, wrapped the tin cup in a towel, and pressed his fingers to the warm sides.

"Now what did you want to ask me, Harry?"

Harry stared at her and tried to keep his face composed. "Nothing," he rasped. "Just... trying to figure out what we did to deserve all this."

Emma's smile illuminated stars and warmed planets—Harry was sure of it. "You boys just... just agreed, Harry. Jumped into my carpet bag as cats and came to start a new life. I just don't want to make you sorry you took a chance on me, you understand?"

Harry nodded and sipped his coffee.

And realized that love came in the strangest of gestures, the most infinitesimal of signs.

THEY REACHED Visalia about an hour before dawn, and Harry urged Suriel to stretch out in the back quarter of the truck.

"Come sleep with me." Suriel yawned. "I'll set wards, Harry—they'll wake you soon enough."

Harry checked in with Edward, who had been dozing for the last hundred miles anyway and was apparently tucked into one of the bedrolls they'd brought. He told Harry he was setting his own wards and then fell back asleep, as a man or a cat, Harry couldn't tell.

"Okay." Harry yawned, trusting. Suriel turned on his side, and Harry went furry and glided up against his chest.

Suriel's hands, stroking his ears back, smoothing his whiskers flat, reassured him on a primal level.

"When we're less tired, I would love to do this with you as a man," Suriel whispered.

Harry lapped delicately at his forearm. Well, yes. But not now. Harry was feeling too raw, too wounded now. He would just appreciate that arm holding him strongly, reminding him that he didn't have to be alone.

Not tonight.

He woke up semipanicked, Suriel's spot next to him cool in the morning chill. Someone was opening the door to the cab, and Harry hissed, skittering back, heart pounding, every alarm in his head going off, when Suriel's voice greeted him.

"I'm sorry, Harry. I went to get you and the boys some chocolate. I hope that's okay."

Harry turned abruptly human, perched on his knees on the uncertain ground of the mattress.

"That's...." Suriel handed him the paper cup, and he took it automatically, smiling shyly into Suriel's eyes. Harry lost the reason he was frightened and upset and took the hot chocolate, dazed and stunned. Suriel's eyes, that warm, rich chocolate brown, mesmerized him.

"That's what?" Suriel asked, teasing.

"You're here," Harry said. "In the morning again. That's wonderful."

Suriel's smile spread, went blinding, and Harry felt as though he'd said something brilliant instead of something obvious.

"I'll go see how the girls are doing." Suriel placed a pastry bag in his hand.

Then Suriel disappeared, closing the door behind him, and Harry was left in the rapidly heating central valley, drinking hot chocolate and remembering the feeling of his fingers wrapped around a towel-insulated tin cup in a drafty cabin next to the ocean.

Harry wasn't stupid. He knew what it was that bound the two memories together.

They twined around his heart as he closed his eyes and sipped his chocolate.

And Harry was no stranger to that taste. He just needed to know how to do for the people who gave him such an elixir to drink.

He was still pondering the question when he slipped out of the truck and went around to find Suriel waiting for him at the back. Harry looked around first, but there'd been no cars in front or behind as he'd pulled off the freeway the night before, and he saw nothing in the school parking lot to make him think any of that had changed.

It was time for the young women he'd been hauling around like so much cargo to see sunlight and remember the joys of being human again.

Harry loved this part.

He unlocked the back and rolled it up, smelling cautiously. They usually brought two or three chemical toilets when they employed the semi, and once one of those things had burst. Sure, Edward and Francis would have warned him—noisily—and insisted they stop and change, as they had before, but Harry had never recovered from unlocking the seal to the stench of hell.

He didn't wake any of the sleepers on the mats in the back of the truck, just let in fresh air and the light of the rising sun.

The first girl to get up—oh, heavens, she looked barely eleven—clung to Francis even as Harry and Suriel lifted their hands to help her hop down. She had dusky skin, a round chin, and dark brown eyes as round as quarters. Someone had braided her long, straight, coarse black hair and trimmed the end with a bedraggled yellow ribbon, and the look she shot Harry from under long bangs was half-afraid, half-delighted.

Harry bent at the knees and winked at her. "You can put the cat down. You know that, right?" he said in Spanish.

She replied in English. "If I do that, the scary boy with the too-white skin will take his place."

Harry held back a chuckle. "Fair enough. Stay right there." He used two hands to vault himself into the truck and started pulling out the camp chairs they stashed in a big box near the door. "Here, Suriel—set these up for them, okay?"

Suriel put the chocolate and pastries down and started taking the chairs and setting them up. Edward stood from his spot in the back, and Harry nodded at the chocolate and pastries.

"Starbucks?" Edward said, sighing. "Oh, I feel so guilty. The girls get donuts as soon as Linda gets here." He yawned and scratched at the back of his head, sending his normally impeccable hair standing straight up. "Where's Francis?"

"Being kept safe from the big scary white man," Harry told him gravely, and Edward's mouth compressed, flashing his dimples.

"Well, that's of critical importance," he said, and while his voice was sober, his eyebrows were *not*, and Harry had to turn away before he burst into laughter.

One at a time, the young women woke up and were helped off the truck. Edward, Harry, and Suriel spent a few moments with each one, finding out if she had any family who would be looking for her, finding out where she most wanted to go.

Most of them *did* have people, and Harry and Edward kept cell phones charged in the front because invariably some of them wanted to call a sister or mother or auntie. The others just shook their heads sorrowfully and looked away.

All of them were assured they'd have a place to go, a job, a home, a shelter.

All of them were told they had a reason to hope.

When the minivans started driving up, Harry and Edward—and Francis, in their heads as he was getting his tummy scritched—had made plans for each girl based on what they'd learned in their short time conversing.

The first van, driven by a woman Harry knew well, came right up front. The woman got out—she was in her fifties now, with a perky red-dyed housewife do and comfortable hips. Harry still remembered when she was a terrified fifteen-year-old hopping out of the back of the U-Haul they'd used back then.

"Harry!" she chirped, trotting to where he stood frantically trying to finish off his pastry. "Edward!"

"Linda!" they cried, and both went in for hugs, and she bussed them on the cheeks for good measure.

"So cute," she said fondly. "And where's Fran—?" Harry pointed to little Inez, Francis still held tight to her chest. "Oh," she murmured. Francis did seem to do that to people. "I see." She grimaced then. "You boys were supposed to be in last night—did anything happen?"

"Not to speak—"

"Yes," Suriel said from Harry's elbow. "This thing they do is dangerous. Harry almost died again."

73

Linda looked concerned but not surprised. "Yes. He got hurt rescuing *me*, as I recall." She smiled sweetly at Suriel. "A long time ago—but the Youngbloods, they gave me a new life." She grabbed Harry's hand and squeezed. "It would be wonderful if they could do it for another hundred years or so, right?"

Harry looked away, embarrassed. Linda had been an accident. Not her rescue—they'd gotten her from a shipment of girls on the East Coast and relocated her in New Mexico with a foster family almost immediately. Twenty years later, she'd heard about an underground network of people helping to rescue and relocate human trafficking victims, and now divorced, with children in middle school, Linda had wanted to help.

Harry had been her contact, and after her initial surprise at seeing him—unaged—she'd laughed quietly to herself. "I saw Edward change into a ginger tomcat when he thought we were sleeping," she'd said, while Harry was still stammering up a lie. "I thought I was imagining it for the last twenty years." Then she'd dimpled at him—still pretty, always irrepressible. "Can *you* turn into anything interesting, Harry?"

Harry had turned cat and wound about her ankles, and she'd been one of their best contacts since.

"We love our jobs," he said, embarrassed. "And I'll try my best."

She rolled her eyes and held her hand out to Suriel. "Linda di Martino. I haven't met you before. Are you and Harry…?" She dimpled again, and Harry laughed, embarrassed.

"Suriel's helping us out for this one run," he said, trying to keep control of the conversation. "But we're happy to have—"

"Just one run?" she asked Suriel, brushing Harry off like any auntie would brush off her nephew, mostly because nephews often lied to keep aunties happy. "The way you're looking at Harry, I'm thinking you'd like more than that."

Suriel ran a possessive hand down Harry's back. Harry gasped and looked at him, helpless to stop any of it—the rush of warmth, the betraying hope, the heart-quaking desire for more. "It's complicated," Suriel understated. "I would, if I could, be with Harry forever—no matter what he chose to do with his time."

Oh heavens. Harry opened his mouth to… to control the conversation, and all that came out was a pitiful meow.

From his very human throat.

Linda turned to him, delight written in the crinkling of the lines around her eyes and the creases around her wide, smiling mouth. "Oh, Harry. You two are so in love I can smell it." She closed her eyes and inhaled briefly. "Eucalyptus, leather, ambergris, and tea."

Harry wrinkled his nose. "Suriel smells like eucalyptus and tea—"

"And you smell like leather and ambergris!" Suriel said happily. "Oh, Linda—what a wonderful gift! Can you do that with everyone?"

She winked. "Sadly, yes. My children have it too—they follow their noses, and it keeps them out of danger." Some of her joy faded, and Harry remembered exactly how Linda had been trapped as a child: she'd found a little boy, used as bait, and "helped" him find his mother.

His "mother" had been one of the most notorious child pornographers of her time.

When she'd finally started talking to adults, she'd told first Harry and then Emma, "How could I know? The little boy smelled like milk… but she… she…."

Harry knew exactly what she'd smelled like; he'd been the one to kill her. It had been milk once—but any mother who's had a kid spill milk in the back of a minivan knows that it goes through a series of smells after that, with vomit being on the high end of the repulsive scale.

That's what evil smelled like.

"Well, I'm sure their mother helps," Harry said kindly.

Linda shook herself. "Speaking of—we have donuts and coffee and hot chocolate in the back. Let me set up—the others are coming."

And sure enough, as she spoke, a few more cars on the road turned into the school.

The next two hours were busy time—all the boys were ready for it. Harry got Inez to put Francis down and go help Linda, and the cat stalked behind a truck and came back, soft brown hair pushed back into a queue, jeans and a blue button-down scrounged hastily from Edward's clothes so he didn't look like the "scary white man" that had so frightened Inez. Francis was as unobtrusive as a human as he was as a cat. Inez was so taken with helping pass out coffee or chocolate, with donuts and fruit for every girl, that she didn't even see him. Some of the other girls looked at him, frowned, spoke to each other, and then frowned again, but none of them pointed their fingers and shouted "Cat!" "Gato!" or "Belyy kot!" so Harry reckoned Francis had been filed away as a hallucinatory part of a generally bad experience.

After over a hundred years doing this, they'd learned that was most often the case.

Their charges had escaped a terrible situation. The hope that it was over took all their strength.

As the temporary foster parents drove up, the boys would tell the escapees about the people they were being matched with: did they have children, what would happen next. Would they be introduced to the legal foster system, or would it be easier to keep them under the radar. Some of the girls were in the country illegally or had parents who weren't citizens yet. Those girls were often too scared to go to the authorities, even if they had a chance to escape, and it was the boys' job to calm them down, convince them that they would just be in the custody of people who wanted what was best for them. Very often, those young people were returned to their families with a minimum of fuss and some contact information to help the girl or boy transition back into their home life.

Sometimes it was easy.

Not always.

Harry and his brothers were the first line of information, letting the people they'd rescued know that it was perfectly fine to be *not* okay.

The work was intense—particularly that first morning, when their charges began to see them as humans, as allies, as people they could go to for help. Edward had produced a pack of specially crafted business cards the boys gave to each evacuee. The cards themselves had a special phone line that Emma and Leonard monitored when the boys were out on a run and the boys monitored frequently when they got back. It wasn't the number that was peculiar about the cards—it was who could see it.

It had taken three tries—and a teeny bit of blood spilled from all the Youngbloods, save Bel—but they'd managed to produce a business card that couldn't be read by a predator. Not just a sexual predator—a political predator, a bully, a blackmailer—anyone who would take advantage of their very particular situation would not be able to see the number on the card.

The cards were hole-punched and put on tiny leather thongs with a charm of safekeeping attached. The charms were tied around the necks of stuffed teddy bears for the especially young charges, and tied around the wrists of the older ones, with the admonition not to lose the number and not to lose the charm.

The charms would keep them safe—or ping the awareness of the Youngblood who had given the charm, should the newly freed prisoner be threatened again. They weren't foolproof. The family couldn't keep everybody safe, no matter how hard they tried.

But the boys could go home after a mission like this one and sleep, knowing they'd done some good in the world.

Most of the time.

John Hartford had been a stunning teenager, with knife-edged cheekbones, black hair, and black-lined brown eyes. As an adult his hair had lightened, and he'd put on enough pleasant roundness for his cheekbones to lose their edge. He looked far more ordinary now, but his shy, happy smile as he welcomed the two boys who'd been with this group was of much better use that day. After some careful questioning—by both Edward *and* Linda—they'd decided John was their best bet.

And he had a concern as well.

"Heya, Harry." John's grip was especially strong. Harry had taught him that as he'd been transitioning to real life over twenty years earlier. John hadn't been forced or trafficked onto the streets. He'd been young and hungry and desperate. Harry had been the one who'd pulled him, sobbing, from a corner of an alleyway as they'd been hustling a roomful of terrified teenagers into a tourist van.

"Nobody made me," he'd gasped. "But I'm so hungry…."

Harry had helped John rescue himself, found him an apartment, gotten him a job, helped him with school.

Turned down—very gently—the advances John had made, long after the hero worship had faded.

Truth was, Harry had liked John too much—but he hadn't loved him. Not enough to give up his immortality or his family, at any rate. But living with him as he grew old and died would have hurt worse than Harry could endure.

John had never met anyone, never married.

But he hadn't grown bitter either.

He'd helped the Youngbloods year after year and said it was the best thing he could do with his life. Harry would do anything he asked.

"Hello, John. Do you have everything you need?"

John looked at the boys—fourteen and fifteen, sober-eyed and terrified.

"I'd better. I have the feeling these two will be with me for a while."

Harry nodded. "Yes, I think so. How's Anya and Krista?"

Four years ago he'd taken in two girls, both of whom would be nearing twenty soon. John had helped both girls start college and learn to live on their own, but he wouldn't have just left them. Not John.

"Anya's missing," John said bluntly, looking like he wanted to cry. "A week ago. She was going to a party, and she told Krista she'd be home by midnight. Two o'clock rolled around and Krista was hysterical. We checked everything—the warehouse where the party took place, the surroundings. I even called the police, but they didn't take it seriously. I tried to explain that this girl wouldn't just go on a bender or take off with a boyfriend, but they weren't buying it." John smiled tiredly. "Krista's been living back with me this last week. She's ready to help with the boys—" He nodded to where his foster daughter was talking to Linda while helping with breakfast cleanup. "—but she's not doing well at all. She and Anya were each other's worlds." Krista, short, stocky, with black hair cut close, looked worried and tired, and Linda was obviously trying to keep up the girl's spirits.

But Harry could see both John and his daughter were trying damned hard to keep their shit together for the two boys they were going to take in.

"I'll call Emma," he said softly. "We'll see what we can do. Our ways might not work, you know, since it's been so long—"

John nodded, eyes bright. "Thanks, Harry. I know this isn't technically your problem, but—"

"You're extended family," Harry said, squeezing his shoulder. "It's absolutely our problem."

John's eyes started to spill, and Harry hugged him tight for a moment, saddened beyond words. Then John pulled back, wiping his eyes, puzzled.

"Harry, why are you calling Emma when she's on her way down? I talked to her last night when she called about the drop. She said she'd be there toward the end. How come you didn't know that?"

Harry's eyes grew so large they lost focus. He blinked a couple of times and turned quickly, finding Edward with a glare.

Edward smiled sweetly, not perturbed in the least. Francis walked up and bumped his elbow, whispering in his ear. Edward nodded, and Francis looked back at Harry and gave a winsome grin, as though he had no idea what Harry could be so upset about, but God knew it wouldn't be anything *they* had done.

"Harry?" John said, a little alarmed.

"Harry." Suriel's voice was more of a caution.

Harry glared at him. "Did you know?"

Suriel didn't look guilty in the least. "Of course I did. I told them to call while you were injured yesterday, because you would need some time."

Harry gaped at him and then turned to John. "John, I promise, someone will help you. I wouldn't just—"

John cocked his head a little sadly at Suriel. "Is that who you've been holding out for?" he asked, the tired lines on his face easing into a melancholy smile. "He's lovely, Harry. I'm flattered you even thought about me at all."

Harry looked at him wretchedly. "You were my very good friend, John. You know tha—"

John held up his hand and then leaned in to kiss him on the cheek. "I do. And I know Edward and Francis can help me look for Anya. If she's there to be found, your family will find her. If she's

79

not...." His voice cracked. "If she's not, I have family to comfort me." He wiped a palm over his eyes. "I'm going to go...." He waved his hand in the direction of Edward and Francis and wandered off. Harry watched him go with an ache in his heart and then rounded on Suriel.

"Was that really necessary?" he asked, guilt pounding him hard. For a moment, just a moment, he'd been excited about spending time with Suriel, just the two of them alone. And then he'd remembered who he was, who *they* were, and how they didn't get vacations.

"It was," Suriel said somberly, putting his hand over Harry's chest. "For this."

"To heal?" He didn't even have a scar from the wound that had shattered his ribs and ripped out part of his lung.

"No. To beat. You cannot keep doing this thing with your family if you don't make your heart whole."

"That man needs me!"

"He does! But if Francis and Edward can't find his daughter, she is not to be found. You know that as well as I do. And in the meantime, there is always one more emergency, isn't there? One more mission. One more lost child you need to save, because the lost child that's inside *you* is still screaming. I may not have long down here, Harry, but by God, you and I are going to *fix* you whether I leave or stay."

And Harry couldn't seem to find words. He opened his mouth and closed his mouth and opened it again.

"So what are you and I...."

Suriel's expression was joy and serenity and self-satisfaction, all rolled into one. "We are going to make love, Harry. I know it's been a while for you, and I've never done it myself, but we're going to let Edward and Francis find Anya, and we're going to have a vacation."

It was like every cell in Harry's brain shorted out. His body lit up, all nerve endings and anticipation, and his brain, his fighting, busy brain, just shut down.

He stared at Suriel, at a loss, and his eyes fixated on, of all things, Suriel's wide, mobile, lush mouth.

Just his mouth.
His lips.
The way they'd felt on Harry's lips, in the desert darkness.
Suriel's smell, eucalyptus and tea.

UNDER ORDERS

HE WAS still gaping at Suriel when the final car rolled up. Most of the rescuers had left with their charges by that time, and only John, his daughter, and Linda and Inez remained.

Suriel looked away, breaking the spell, and a great smile took over his face, the expression Suriel reserved for one person in the world.

"Oh hell," Harry grunted, finally noticing the brand-new Honda Odyssey. "Emma and Leonard are here."

Francis walked up behind him and bumped shoulders. "You like seeing them," he said quietly. Then *he* started to radiate the same sunshine joy Suriel was. "Bel!" he cried. "Beltane—they brought him!"

Francis rushed to the Odyssey waving his arms and jumping up and down, showing more emotion in that moment than he did during an entire year *not* in Bel's company. Edward wandered up and eyed him with the same uneasiness Harry showed.

"That... that is very interesting," he said softly.

"It's been that way since Beltane was born," Harry replied. He smiled to himself. "I think I heard him say once that Bel was his reward for remembering how to be human."

Edward grunted. "He doesn't do that good a job being human. I think he should just get dessert or something."

"That's not fair!" Harry countered. He thought back to when Francis was a child, when Edward and Harry spent all their days working as hard as possible to keep him from the ugliness their lives had become. Francis had been wide-eyed then and perfectly happy to look away—a magician's perfect assistant, the gullible audience, willing to be fooled. "He's been fey his whole life. Bel was just... just the human he chose to live with, is all."

"Is this about driving away the brownies?" Edward asked suspiciously. "They were drinking all of Leonard's beer. And the hill in Foresthill is a better place for them—you know that."

"I liked them," Harry snapped. "They were good sports to hunt, and sometimes they hunted back. But that's not the point."

"Then what *is* the point? Why are you so pissed off?"

Harry glared at him, hurt all over again. "You made arrangements to go... go do whatever. Without me. I don't get to hunt with you anymore?"

"That's not what this is," Edward said, his rolled eyes speaking to exaggerated patience. "Of course we want you with us. It's the family business, Harry—you're part of the family. We called Emma and Leonard because you're using it as an excuse." Emma had pulled to a halt, and she and Leonard got out and were stretching cautiously. In order to have Bel, she and Leonard had both given up a portion of their power. The magic that kept them from aging was not quite as strong as it had been so long ago.

"More like twenty years in a hundred," Emma had said when she'd told the boys of their plan to conceive a child. "Unlike the ten or so you boys will continue to age." Francis had regarded her with avid, crossed blue eyes, his tail twitching, since he'd refused to change forms for the family meeting. "Or *five* in a hundred, for those of us who prefer to be cats," she'd added acidly.

Because Francis was Francis, his back leg had shot up, and he'd given her a pointed demonstration of his position on the subject.

But twenty years later, the results of that consultation could be seen. Emma, who had always been a mostly ageless-appearing woman in her late twenties, was now most definitely in her late thirties, with fine lines around her eyes and deeper grooves at the mouth. Her hair—still blonde and thick and lovely—now had a few strands of silver in it. She was still beautiful, and the kindness in her eyes, her smile, had never diminished.

But she appeared human now, vulnerable, and today she looked worried.

Her eyes sought out Harry as soon as she'd straightened from her stretch. She said a few words to Leonard, who eyed Harry up and down too and shook his head.

"I think she's annoyed." Edward clapped him on the shoulder. "Well done!"

"Look, if even one of you had said anything to me beforehand—"

And suddenly Edward wasn't laughing anymore. "When, Harry? When you were throwing yourself at one job after another? When you were bleeding out? No job was too dangerous, remember? 'We've got an advantage and a moral obligation to use it in the pursuit of justice and compassion,' remember that?"

"Nicely spoken," Suriel said warmly. "When was that?"

"Right before we took this one on," Edward told him sourly. "Francis had done some scouting and reported over twenty guards and five vehicles. We were going to hold out for Emma and Leonard, but Hero here couldn't wait for anybody, could he?"

Harry couldn't look at Edward as his words came back to haunt him. "Damned hubris," he muttered. "Always comes back to bite you in the—"

Edward shoved him. "Not hubris," he said, voice bitter. "Self-annihilating pain. If Suriel hadn't come to bail you out, we would have held the intervention ourselves."

Harry looked away, unable to summon an argument for that. "I'm sorry, my brother." He bit his lip and in that moment felt every mortal year of two lifetimes on his shoulders. "I'll try to remember myself from now on. I shouldn't put you and Francis into danger because—"

Edward swung at him, and Suriel stopped him, holding his fist before it struck home on Harry's jaw.

"No," Suriel said, voice of quiet thunder. "Not even you."

Edward fought tears for a moment and then slouched in defeat, arm falling limply to his side. "Don't be sorry," he said after a few moments of absolute silence. "Don't be sorry. Be *happy*. Find your joy, Harry. Live your long life with us and be happy."

And with that he pivoted on his heel and stalked to the minivan, throwing himself into Emma's hug without restraint.

Harry saw his shoulders shake for a moment, and his heart twisted a little tighter. "I haven't seen him cry in ages." Edward *had* taken lovers, two of them. Allan had died of a brain hemorrhage at sixty-two. Dorothy had died in a polio epidemic when she'd been only twenty-one. Edward had taken both deaths hard—had cried unashamedly on his family—and then, when his mourning was over, had spent years of time with Mullins, making things right again in his heart.

He was crying on Emma as though he was mourning Harry already.

"He can't lose me," Harry said in wonder. "He can't...."

"This life you all live, outside the mortal boundaries—it's hard on you in ways a mortal life isn't," Suriel told him.

Harry had heard this lesson a hundred or so times. "I must be very thick," he realized. "I think this is the first time I really understood what that means."

Suriel turned and wrapped his arms around Harry's shoulders, and Harry didn't fight him, didn't ask why. He simply melted into Suriel's touch and surrendered, an exhaustion so marrow-deep and heart-long he hadn't known he'd borne it draining from his body.

"What am I going to do?" He was too tired and hurt to be anything but honest. "What am I going to do when I can never see you again?"

"Harry?"

Only Emma's voice could have made him stir. Harry pulled away from Suriel and found his mother's arms wrapped securely around him.

"Sorry to worry you," he said gruffly. He looked over Emma's shoulder and smiled apologetically at Leonard. "I know how much you hate to travel."

Leonard rolled his eyes. "It's more frightening when your mother drives."

Some of his exhaustion fell away. He straightened and kissed Emma on the cheek. "You didn't need to come down," he said doggedly. "Suriel and the boys talked some sense—oolf!"

Beltane appeared out of nowhere and hugged Harry for all he was worth.

"Holy beefsteak, Bel Youngblood! You can let go before you crack my ribs!"

Bel stepped back and grinned, his outsized biceps and broad shoulders dwarfing Harry as he dwarfed Edward and Francis. In Harry's day, the three of them were moderately tall, standing between Francis's five feet five and Edward's five feet eight.

Bel Youngblood passed Edward up during his first growth spurt. He passed his father—who stood over six feet tall—during his last one, at the end of what would have been high school, had he ever attended.

"All I know is that everybody's mad at you," Bel said blithely. "I know when everybody is mad at *me*, a solid hug always makes it better."

Harry grinned up at him, entranced as everybody else had been over their baby, their perfect child. "When, in your entire life, has anybody been mad at *you*?" he asked teasingly.

Bel had the grace to look away, and Emma scowled furiously. Even Leonard looked irritated, and he was the family rock.

Harry's family antennae perked right up. "What?"

"You tell him," Emma snapped to Bel. "I just—" Her hands flailed expressively, and Harry read her loud and clear.

"Jesus, boy—tell us before she explodes!"

"I'm not going to Oxford," Bel said shortly, glaring at his mother.

Harry's mouth fell open. "But Bel—you… you told your mother years ago, you were going to spend five years at Oxford and then come home. There's a wizard there who can teach you, and peers, on both sides of the divide. Why would you—"

"He can't bring cats," Emma muttered. "Of all the stubborn, shortsighted—"

Harry blinked at him and for the first time realized Bel's handsome, rectangular face and deep hazel eyes could look stubborn and determined, much like his mother's—or his father's, for that matter.

"I won't leave him," Bel said. He scowled at Harry. "Are *you* going to try to talk me out of it?"

Harry shook his head and held out his hands. "I've had enough of that crap this morning to last me another two lifetimes," he said, sincerity rocking from the bottom of his toes. "You make the decisions best for you and your heart, Bel. You know I'll always love you."

He and the others had listened to Bel making excited vowels as he lay on a play blanket in a sunny room. They'd helped him take his first steps, had played with him—mostly as cats—when he'd been restless or teething, and had helped him learn his letters, and his figures, and chemistry and biology—and magic.

He could remember his delight the first time Bel had changed shape, and Francis's pique when the shape had turned out to be a big blond dog.

Francis had overcome his disappointment, though, and soon he and Bel had become legendary in their county as the white cat and the yellow dog, and together the two of them had probably had adventures that would age Emma twenty years in a night—if only they told.

"I love you too," Bel said, giving his mother the side-eye. "And I'm not going to nag you."

"Well, I'm very grate—"

"I'm just going to tell you that now that I'm grown, I have an abominably long time on the planet, and you are one of the people I count on being there for the entire damned millennia. Do what you have to for that to happen, do you understand? This is bullshit. Mom and I were in the middle of a rip-roaring fight and suddenly we're tearing ass down the road. We haven't even stopped for dinner! Or breakfast! Or snack! Or coffee! Or—"

Francis appeared at his elbow with a pink box full of donuts, and Bel shoved one in his mouth.

"Fixth ith," he ordered direly as Francis pulled him away.

Harry watched as he and Francis helped Linda clean up the last of the breakfast and saw that Edward was getting information from John and Krista.

He sighed and turned to his mother. "Fine," he said. "I already told Suriel I'd go, but I think you're all—"

"I love you, Harry, but you're full of shit. Leonard, give me your hand—the cabin by the house, you think?"

Leonard smiled. "It's already stocked, dearest. Harry?"

"Leonard, I haven't even had time to say hello to you—"

"I love you, son. Your mother's right. Your mother's always right." Leonard stepped in and hugged him tight. "Love finds a way," he whispered. "Through years, through death, through magic portals to hell. Believe in it, okay?"

"Of course." Because Harry loved this man more than he'd ever loved his own father. "For you and Emma—"

Emma grabbed Leonard's hand. "We'll be there in four days. Suriel, try to stick around until then."

"Of course, Emma," Suriel said dryly.

Emma glared at him. "And if you actually *do* disappear forever, I will stalk into heaven and drag you out by the fucking ear. This isn't goodbye. I don't do goodbyes."

Leonard cleared his throat and looked at Harry and Suriel, eyes dancing.

Emma glared at him too. "I do 'see you later.'" She waved imperiously with her free hand. "See you idiots later."

"Emma, this isn't ne—"

Harry's ears popped, and he yawned. When he recovered from the yawn, he opened his eyes and saw that, sure as the sun was warm and water wet, he and Suriel were in the family cabin. Placed a few miles from the house, it sat right next to a tributary stream and consisted of one room, much like the room the original house had started out as.

It was small, cozy, stocked with food and spare clothes, and bless Leonard, heated.

"Why didn't she just let us drive back?" Suriel asked, yawning too. "That's disconcerting."

"Because this way *she* has the minivan to carry people around after they ditch the truck," Harry told him sourly. "And also because she likes to show off, and she's not great at doing that for herself. She disappeared for a month once, and Leonard had to scry for her. We ended up in the middle of a war zone in Central America to fetch her— he was pissed."

"Probably best it was us, then." Suriel looked around at the wood-paneled walls and the thick wool rugs under their feet. "Oh look! Emma's watercolors," he said with joy, seeing the complex, lovely artwork framed on the far wall. "She does love her seascapes."

In fact, she made money in the summer selling her artwork—and her weaving and handspun yarn—in a booth in downtown Mendocino. It didn't make her much, certainly not compared to the money she and Leonard brought in with investments, but it made her happy.

"I tried to paint once," Harry said, gathering clothes. The cabin had a couch in front of a television on one end and a queen-sized bed with a dresser kitty-corner to it, all the woodwork simple and sturdy. Leonard was a craftsman at heart. The kitchenette—with a refrigerator and stocked shelves of dry goods—stood at the far end, near the door. The bathroom attached to the house, like a little pod with a tiled floor, shower, and a toilet—and a spa-sized bathtub, complete with waterjets and bath salts.

"Oh yes?" Suriel looked over his shoulder at Harry and smiled. "I didn't know this."

Harry shrugged. "I had no knack for it. Emma's work was so... so delicate. So lovely. I didn't want to paint if I couldn't paint like that."

Suriel's brows arched together again, that thoughtful line appearing. "Harry...." Then he took in what Harry was actually doing. "You're going to take a bath?"

"A shower—I'm feeling a bit grimy. You can have it after me if...." He frowned and noticed Suriel's wings for the first time that day. "Do you, uh... I mean, you wanted to jump in the watering hole, but... uh, I'm not sure where you are in your, uh...."

Suriel's smile turned mysterious. Sultry. "Go shower, Harry. I assure you, I'll fit fine."

"I'll be out in a few," Harry said uncertainly.

Suriel's eyes did that thing where they widened at the outside corners. It made Suriel look... well, less than angelic, really. "You do what you need to do," he said blandly.

Harry regarded him with deep-seated uneasiness. "You're plotting something. I don't know what it is, but we'll discuss it when I get out."

Suriel nodded as though that was perfectly acceptable. "Of course. But while you're in there, I want you to ask yourself something."

"Fine. What?"

"Exactly what did I tell you was going to happen this week?"

For a moment, Harry saw him—*him*. Long, elegant body, square jaw, pointed chin, warm, fathomless brown eyes. *He* wasn't an angel anymore, he was a *man*, and he'd kissed Harry senseless not twelve hours earlier.

His entire body flushed hot, his neck sweating,

"Nungh!" Harry rushed to the bathroom, within an arm's breadth of Suriel himself, in an effort to get out of there.

He ran the water and stripped quickly, then found a bath sponge and some of Emma's homemade bath soap in a bottle. Emma—bless her—had ceded to living with five men and become an expert in finding smells that weren't too flowery or overwhelming.

This one smelled like leather and ambergris, and the irony was not lost on Harry.

He'd soaped everything twice and was rinsing his hair when a burst of cool air made him blink against the water. The shower door had opened, and a warm male body, one taller than average when Harry was shorter, slid into the cubicle behind Harry.

"It's me," Suriel said unnecessarily.

Harry swallowed, throat dry. "I knew that." He closed his eyes, and Suriel wrapped warm fingers around his hips and pulled him back, unresisting, until he could feel all of Suriel's long, fine body along his backside.

Disregarding the pounding water, Suriel lowered his mouth to Harry's ear. "Are you nervous, Harry?"

His whole life, he'd never been anything but honest with this man. "Yes." He shuddered, and want raced down his nerve endings.

"Why? Why would you be afraid of me?"

Honesty. It would kill him.

"I…." He took a deep breath and tried again. His family had accused him of fear—he needed to speak his heart unafraid. "I wanted you," he rasped. "I wanted you that first night. But I was a *whore*, Suriel. And I didn't want that thing… that thing that was done to me to be anywhere near you."

Suriel held him tighter, arms wrapping around his chest. "I know Emma taught you better than that since then."

Harry smiled slightly. "Of course she did. Sex can be really amazing." He closed his eyes and remembered John, how beautiful he'd been as a youngster, what a kind man he was now. "But it's... it's not something I've ever done with someone I could care for. Because I knew I could lose that person. And now...." His voice trembled, broke. "Now you're asking me to... to...."

"Make love," Suriel whispered in his ear. "We're going to make love. It's like having sex, but I've loved you since you were a confused tomcat on a very eventful night. I've had the privilege of watching you grow into a beautiful man, of watching you strive hard to do good every day of a very long life. Do you think I love you less now than on that day?"

Harry could hardly breathe. "I only wanted to be worthy of my angel."

"You're so worthy." Suriel's voice wobbled too. "You're worth falling. You're worth pain. You're worth giving up my station in heaven and coming down to live a mortal life, if only I'm allowed. Please, Harry—believe me. I've never met a more worthy man."

Harry turned in his arms and buried his face against Suriel's chest. When he spoke again, his voice seemed to echo from far away. "And now you want me, and you're going to teach me all about what love should feel like, and you're going to *leave*. Oh God... oh, Suriel—you thought I feared Cass. It's nothing to what... what I feel... when I think of being here alone without you!"

Suriel's own breath sobbed hotly in Harry's ear. "And you're going to face the fear all mortals face, Harry. And you're going to do it beautifully. Because if you don't face *this* fear, you will have to live your whole long life never knowing what love is." His voice rose. "And *that* is unacceptable. I would bear a thousand years of torture, just to know my boy knew love."

Harry pulled back enough to look up to see the lines of desperation and desire etched cleanly along Suriel's cheekbones and the corners of his eyes. He was beautiful—still beautiful—but he looked powerful and grief-stricken in ways Harry had never fathomed.

Harry reached up to cup his cheek, feeling the heat of tears there, even if the water still coursed down. "Don't cry," he begged. "Don't cry for me, my angel."

Anything, anything but to cause Suriel grief.

Suriel cupped his cheek in turn, rubbing the tears away before the shower could. "What would you have me do, brave Harry? Give me something to do besides weep."

Harry wanted to close his eyes, but Suriel was holding him as a man and looking at him with passion in his brown eyes. He'd been asked to be brave, to fight his fears, and he'd been fighting his whole life.

He thought that's what he'd have to do.

But looking into the face of a weeping angel, he took a deep breath and did the unthinkable: he submitted. He gave in to the will of his heart, of Suriel's love.

He submitted to loving a man, and losing him, and knowing the joy of love along the way.

Suriel's grief eased, and he stroked Harry's cheek again. "What would you have me do?" he repeated—but this time he sounded like he knew.

"Love me," Harry whispered. "Love me, Suriel. Teach me what it is to love with all my heart."

A smile broke through, sunshine through clouds. "You already know. You've known for years. But here I am, in a corporeal body, and I have never felt the stirrings of blood under skin until I kissed you under a starry sky. It's you who must teach me."

Harry cupped both his cheeks, stroking them in wonder. No beard stubble—not for his angel—and no roughness. Just silken skin and that surprisingly firm jaw. Harry stretched up on his toes and pulled Suriel down to meet him in a kiss.

Suriel groaned and lifted him up, supernatural strength making it easy for him to wrap two long-fingered hands around Harry's muscled thighs so Harry could twine his legs around that slender waist. Their bodies, wet and slick, slid together, hot and needy, and Harry could have cried with the lack of friction. He tore his mouth away from Suriel's and reached behind him, fumbling to turn off the spigot.

"Bed," he ordered.

Suriel laughed throatily. "Towels," he added. "And...."

Harry pulled back to see what made him pause. "Suriel?"

"Something slippery," Suriel managed to say with dignity. "For, uh, penetration."

Harry felt a wicked smile curve his lips. "Lubricant, Suriel. We've been calling it lubricant for years. There's usually some in the drawers here."

Suriel frowned and kissed along Harry's jaw before asking, "Why is there a sexual aid in your parents' cabin, Harry?"

Harry tilted back his head and let Suriel's lips move on his ear, his neck—the vulnerable places he'd spent two lifetimes protecting suddenly open, accepting as they'd never been before. "Maybe for my parents," he said, not thinking about it too hard. "Maybe for Edward—he takes lovers here sometimes."

Suriel moved to Harry's collarbone, licking a line to his shoulder, and Harry bucked against him, willing him to hurry. The cabin wasn't that big! Harry wanted to be splayed on the bed, licked and stretched, accepting and ready, as soon as possible.

It was a thing he'd never allowed a lover to do to him.

Suriel would take care of him. Suriel had apparently been waiting a very long time to do just that.

True to his promise, he held Harry one-handed, taking his mouth again. Still kissing, he carried Harry—dripping and wet—to the bed in the corner of the cabin's main room. The kiss continued, ravenous, never-ending, while he pulled the covers back. Then he set Harry down and grabbed one of two towels draped over the end of the bed to dry Harry off as he sat.

Harry rough-dried his sopping wet hair, then his torso, and then Suriel took the towel from him and began working on his own hair—but apparently he was still mulling the private lives of all the people Harry loved.

"Do you think Bel and Francis come here?" he asked, puzzled.

Harry had snagged the other towel and begun working on his thighs and creases. He paused then, gaping at Suriel in confusion.

"Bel? Francis?"

Suriel shook his hair out and ruffled his wings. The hair flew out, lank and still damp, like any human's. The wings flicked water in a fine mist and then returned to their normal diaphanous semisolid dream state.

He looked at Harry's shock and ran fingertips down his cheek. "They've become lovers this last year—I thought you knew."

"No," Harry said numbly, trying hard not to think about what that would do to their family.

Suriel sank to a crouch and ran his fingertips over Harry's thighs. "You're the first to fall, but hardly the only one, Harry. Why do you think your brothers want you settled so badly?"

Harry gasped as Suriel bent his head and replaced the wandering of his fingers with the silken tenderness of his lips.

"They're waiting for me?" he gasped. His cock swelled, grew hard and aching, and Suriel teased his flanks, his hip bones, his thighs—everywhere but his genitals, the place he'd been sure sex was all about.

"You're the last and the first." Suriel looked up with a lick of his lips. "Are you ready?"

"Gah!" Harry ran his fingers through Suriel's hair, untangling the wet strands, shuddering at the sensuality of having it dry and sliding against itself like raw satin.

"For me, Harry," Suriel teased, flicking his tongue out to barely tease Harry's cockhead. "Your family can wait."

"Good," Harry said shortly, fighting not to arch his hips up and simply ravish Suriel's mouth. "For right now, it's just you and me."

"Always," Suriel promised. "Here, touching skin, we're the only two people in the world."

His breath alone was like the brush of a feather. Harry keened, bucking because he couldn't stand it any longer. "Suriel—oh God... touch me!"

Suriel spread his hand on Harry's chest and pushed him gently backward. "Spread your legs," he ordered, and Harry put both his feet up on the edge of the bed, his thighs spread wide. His barest, most vulnerable bits were on display, cooling slightly in the open air as he dried, and Suriel crouched a little lower, spreading his cheeks and blowing.

Harry closed his eyes. His body vibrated, so needy, hungry for an act he'd never experienced for his own pleasure.

Suriel seemed to know this. He plied his tongue along Harry's taint for a moment and then dipped it lower, burrowing. Harry gasped, making a whimpering sound he'd never associated with himself and sex, and Suriel spread his hand again, pressing against Harry's abdomen, making him flatten his hips against the mattress.

"I know you need," he said, nuzzling Harry's thigh. "I know you. This thing I'm going to do—where I'm going to go—this isn't something you let yourself do." He raised his face just enough for Harry to see a sweet smile. "Not trusting, my Harry. But you trust me."

Harry nodded, his skin prickling with unanswered need.

"I do."

Suriel spread him wide again, licked, softly first, then aggressively, and Harry closed his eyes and allowed himself to fall.

That insistent pressure, that wet, lovely softness, and then up... up... engulfing his testicles gently, then a long, delirious swipe from his base to his wet and aching bell.

Harry wanted to sob. His body blazed with desire, with need, and Suriel was exploring, nuzzling, and he had one thing to do. No fighting, no pursuing, no deciding—he had to abandon himself to Suriel's ministrations and believe that someone cared enough about him to do what Harry needed most.

Harry had never fathomed how much he needed Suriel's hands and mouth and tongue.

Ah! A finger penetrated him, then two, while Suriel's other hand wrapped around his cock and stroked. Harry crossed his arms over his face, hiding from the sunlight, giving his whole being permission to be washed away in the onslaught of sensation.

Suriel's mouth—treacherous, evil mouth, for an angel—sucked harder, played with his bell, the sensitive underside, the slit. Harry groaned, bucking off the bed because he had no choice. "Suriel, I'm going to... I'm... oh God, please—"

Suriel thrust hard into his backside and took him down to the root.

Harry cried out, grabbing the sheets on either side and letting the light of climax wash over him. A searing, scalding path of orgasm bolted through his body, and he clung to the blankets, to the feeling of Suriel's hot mouth, his clever fingers, to help remind him who he was.

The giant wave receded, but he wasn't out of hot water yet. His back end still ached, sensitized, needing, and his cock softened slightly but not entirely.

As the last shudder racked him, he found his body still trembling, still aroused to the point of pain.

"Suriel!" he sobbed. "Suriel, I can't—"

Then Suriel withdrew his fingers and pushed up on the bed, covering Harry's body and settling his hips between Harry's thighs. Harry grunted and wrapped his legs around Suriel's thighs in an attempt to get closer.

"Shh…." Suriel covered Harry's mouth with his own, and Harry tried to climb inside the comfort of the kiss. Suriel leaned back and regarded him soberly, arching his back and pushing his erection against Harry's. "Are you ready?"

Harry was crawling out of his skin. "Please…."

"I'm going to be inside you, and I'm going to fill the empty places. And even if I go, you'll know I'll always be in your heart."

Harry nodded, closing his eyes, and Suriel nipped at his chin.

"Look at me, Harry. Watch me do this. I'm just as human as you."

Harry's eyes flew open just as Suriel positioned himself, biting his lip in concentration. Some of the intensity eased from the moment, and Harry said, "It's not rocket scie—ahhhh…."

Suriel thrust inside.

Such a mundane human concept, stimulating nerve endings with an appropriately shaped object to inspire pleasure.

Such a stunning, glorious melding of pain and pleasure, sensation and sense, heart and body, as Suriel filled him, inch by all-consuming inch. Harry moaned, he gibbered, and then as Suriel seated himself completely, he screamed.

Suriel pulled out, and the emptiness consumed him.

"Again," he panted. "Please, Suriel, again!"

Suriel rocked forward more quickly this time, and Harry saw stars as he bottomed out. Again and again and again, and Harry could do nothing but clutch him closer, clawing at his shoulders and upper arms.

"Look at me," Suriel commanded. "See me!"

His voice didn't thunder, didn't echo, but Harry forced his eyes open, compelled because his lover asked him and he wanted to please.

Suriel's head tilted back, his eyes half-closed, and the cords on his neck and chest stood out as he supported himself on the bed. His teeth were pulled back in a snarl, and he chased his own orgasm as relentlessly as Harry ever had during sex.

He was human, a person, a lover in Harry's bed, a cock in his body—a pure shining soul in Harry's heart.

"Suriel!" Harry gasped, and Suriel lowered his head and met Harry's eyes. "I see you! I see you!"

A kiss then, ravening, starved, as Suriel's hips pumped continuously, seeking oblivion.

"I see you too, brave Harry."

Ah! Ah! Right there! Suriel's body pushed up against Harry's erection, and his cock inside Harry's body found the spot, the place that sent another shower of sparks behind Harry's eyes. "I see you," Harry gasped again. "I see you. You're beautiful."

Suriel cried out, swelling against Harry's opening, and Harry gripped him tight. Suriel gasped, in the throes of the short, hard thrusts that would bring him to climax.

"Harry!" He sounded frightened.

Oh, Harry's angel—this was so new, so overwhelming.

Harry cupped his neck then and thrust back against him. "Suriel, I see you. Come for me, my lover. Come inside me. Make me yours!"

A slow, beatific smile spread over Suriel's features, and time banked, crested. Stood still.

Broke ponderously, pleasure crashing over the both of them like a leviathan wave, and Harry finally closed his eyes as his whole body became the fiery white light of come. Suriel pumped orgasm into Harry's body, and Harry whispered nonsense words in his ear.

"I love you, my angel. I love you. I love your sweat and your come. I love you inside me. I love you in my heart. I love you, Suriel. Don't ever leave me. I need you right here. Don't ever leave."

Suriel sagged into him, let Harry bear his full weight. Harry fought to breathe, fought to keep him, right there where he belonged.

Finally he spoke, nuzzled Harry's cheek, whispered in his ear. "I love you, brave Harry. And if I'm ever called from your side—"

"No!" Harry protested, already bereft.

"You need to remember." Suriel pushed up on his elbows, his body sliding from Harry's and leaving him cold and empty.

"Remember what?" Harry asked wretchedly.

"That I will be battling everything. I will be fighting heaven and hell to come back to your side. Can you remember that?"

And the warmth seeped back into Harry's heart. "I hate that you'd be in pain," he confessed. "I was trying to give you up, just so you wouldn't have to be in pain."

"Too late." Suriel rubbed his lips along Harry's cheekbone. "Probably the moment I arrived was too late, but I didn't want to admit it. The moment we first kissed was my last chance to turn back, and I wouldn't have done it for all the peace in heaven. But now, definitely now, it's too late. Any pain. Any fear. Any fight. It's worth it, Harry. For one more moment touching skin to skin."

Harry bit his lip and nodded. Lovers had been making vows like this from the beginning of time, but from Suriel, the words had greater weight. Harry would never forget that moment he'd first seen what the Angel Who is Bound endured to alleviate the suffering of those who were bound against their will.

All these years and so many fears.

What Harry had feared most had been what Suriel would endure to be at Harry's side.

"I'd do anything," he said, even as Suriel slid off his body and propped himself on his side, head resting on his hand. "Anything to spare you that."

Suriel's smile held weariness and forgiveness both. "Including put this moment off for a hundred and thirty years," he murmured, tracing idle patterns on Harry's chest.

Harry looked at him curiously. "Would you really?" he asked, the pain of that time denied almost strangling him. "Would you really have risked everything to be with me back then?"

Suriel thought about it in all seriousness. "I would have," he said, and Harry's heart fell. "But it wouldn't have worked then."

"Why not?" Harry summoned enough control over his replete limbs to roll to his side so they could be face-to-face. Suriel's hair spilled over his hand and pooled on the sheet beneath him. His body, long and pale, fine and defined, stretched out, compelling Harry's touch. He ran his hand along his narrow flank and smiled slightly when Suriel gasped and drew up his arm protectively. "Ticklish?" he asked.

"Apparently so!" The delight in his voice!

"I'll be sure to tickle you," Harry promised, breaking into a full-fledged grin. He sobered, though. "But you need to answer my question."

Suriel seized his hand and squeezed. "I would have made love to you and never regretted it," Suriel said, looking troubled. "It's how angels created the Nephilim, you know."

"I did not." Harry didn't think he *could* be surprised.

"They come down from heaven and make love to humans— much like elves do, come to think about it." Suriel rolled his eyes. "The children of the divine, always playing with humans and breaking their toys. Anyway, I could have done that. Made love to you, put up a petty rebellion, tried to break away from my station and fallen."

Harry regarded him soberly. "You don't think you would have succeeded?"

"No," Suriel said decisively. He traced the firm line of Harry's jaw. "Because I hadn't seen you suffer yet. Hadn't seen you try so hard to not call me, hadn't felt your heartache from heaven, wanting me by your side. You've been bound by love to me for over a century, Harry, and you denied it every day so I wouldn't be in pain. How can I not return to you now, after seeing that? You were dying breath by breath, tempting fate every day, because you didn't want to live without me. If I had to go back up to heaven now and stay, never to see you again until you died, ripping you from your family, I'm not sure whose pain would unmake me first—yours or my own. No. A hundred and thirty years ago, I would not have believed enough in you to break from my post and fall for our lifetime together. But today—today, you can have faith."

Harry's lips were parted and dry, and he licked them as he thought. "That's…." His mouth quirked. "All these years, I assumed I wasn't enough."

"*I* wasn't enough, brave Harry. But now I am. And I want you. I want our lives together, however long they may be. And our deaths together, and all the time after that."

The warmth in Harry's chest grew painful, hot, and it spilled over from his eyes. "In this family, you have no idea how long that'll be," he said, trying to hold his voice firm. Suriel must have seen right through him, though, because in a breath, he looped an arm around Harry's shoulders and pulled him tight against his chest.

And Harry wept for the two of them together, and the hope, and the joy of what could be.

In the Time It Takes to Blossom

THE CABIN windows were closed, and the cabin grew warm and stuffy in the afternoon heat. Harry awoke from a dream in which he was stifled against a silken pillow only to find himself sweating and sticking to Suriel, skin on skin.

Harry peeled himself away carefully and opened all the windows, moving like a shadow. With the first waft of sea-scented breeze, some of the tension in his shoulders eased.

He opened the front door and let the breeze hit his bare body without impediment, raising his arms and turning his face toward the late-afternoon sun.

He felt Suriel's heat before he heard any moving about, but still, he was not surprised at the hands spanning his midriff and pulling him back into his lover's chest.

"Mm...."

Suriel nuzzled the hollow of his neck, and Harry hummed, clasping the arms under his ribs and abandoning himself to the touch.

"Regrets?" Suriel asked.

"I should ask you," Harry said. "You're the one who lost his virginity."

Suriel's filthy chuckle warmed him. "Well, yes, I suppose in a way."

"If you want to lose it in the other way, let me know," Harry said playfully. Then he paused. "Unless that's... I don't know. Forbidden angel sex or something."

Suriel laughed louder this time, whole body vibrating. "No, not that I know of. As far as I know, all forms of consensual intercourse constitute the loss of one's virginity."

Harry frowned. "Not nonconsensual?"

"No," Suriel said softly. "Sex is a gift—not a requirement. If the gift doesn't appeal to you, it becomes a burden. If it's forced upon you, it's a violation."

Oh. How, in all their midnight talks, had that never come up?

"You're thinking about your childhood, aren't you?" Suriel asked into the suddenly uncomfortable silence.

"A brothel, Suriel."

"My brave boy, protecting his brothers."

Harry did an amazing thing then, his lover holding him, naked to the sun and the sky and the green meadow and the running spring. He let it go.

"I was a virgin, then. The farrier's boy who seduced me, maybe five years after moving here—he was my first."

"Was he kind?"

Harry laughed. "Enthusiastic. But fair-handed." Mostly the fair-handed had been his trick, stroking them both off at once.

Suriel's laugh was unfettered. "Sounds lovely. The lovers you chose on your own, Harry—those lovers are yours to keep in your heart. Does that bother you?"

Harry didn't even have to think. "No," he said, closing his eyes. "All I learned from them, I brought here, for today. It was my best time."

Suriel held him tighter. "I would like more."

Harry turned his head and smiled shyly. "Yes, but not just yet." He sniffed the breeze, full of game and wind and promise. "Suriel, would you like to hunt with me?"

Suriel's "Oooh…." of gratification was all he needed. Harry shifted and took a few delicate, questioning steps out of the cabin. He felt the rush of displaced air and smelled the giant hunting cat and turned his head to see Suriel in his furry form.

Would you like to hunt or play? The question was serious. They could bring down game in these forms, but the fridge was also fully stocked with steaks, mushrooms, and potatoes.

Play, Suriel said promptly.

And Harry took off running, heading for the nearest tree to climb, Suriel at his heels.

There are no rules to cat play. They climbed the tree and chased one another, the chaser changing to the chased on the turn of the breeze. Suriel, true to his Maine coon roots, leaped into the slow-moving stream, probably intending to frolic for a bit. Only his yowl revealed that he wasn't prepared for the thrill of the cold water, and Harry stayed up in his tree and laughed madly—until Suriel glared at the limb he was on and it broke, sending Harry into the water in a mad flurry of hissing.

He flailed for a moment, trying the time-honored cat method of walking on top of the stuff before conceding that he would have to swim it after all.

He paddled a bit, irritated and spoiling for a fight, until he realized that Suriel, grown used to the temperature by now, was actually enjoying himself, swimming to the narrow part of the stream and letting the current carry him down, diving under the water, and at one point fishing good-naturedly for minnows.

Harry gave up on his cat prejudices and found the shallows, sitting on his haunches and splashing experimentally while Suriel did the more advanced cat-swimming maneuvers in the deeper end.

Eventually Suriel joined him just as Harry pulled out a minnow, wiggling on his claw.

Suriel meowed questioningly and opened his mouth.

Harry put his paw in Suriel's mouth and let him eat the minnow, which he did with a flourish.

All we need now are the loaves, Suriel said smugly, and Harry rolled his mental eyes at the awfulness of the joke.

Seriously—we need to either bring down a rabbit or go cook a steak, Harry told him.

Suriel bopped him on the nose with a wet paw, and Harry jumped on top of him. They rolled and tussled for a moment until Suriel had Harry on his back, glaring, because submission was something Harry had only done in bed, once, not hours before.

Harry panted and opened his teeth in a feline grin before shifting forms. As a naked man on his back, he wrapped his arms around the great big cat on his chest and squeezed affectionately. "Now, I love you, but I'm getting hungry. I get foul when I get hungry, and you shouldn't be made to see that."

Suriel licked his chin, rough tongue rasping against whiskers Harry hadn't shaved in a couple of days. "You like this form, do you?" Harry asked.

Suriel purred.

"Well then, back to the house, and you can play with the dust bunnies while I cook." Harry changed and prowled through the long meadow grass back to the cabin, Suriel swatting at butterflies behind him. The long shadows of summer evening stretched over them from the direction of the ocean, and Harry's whiskers twitched in the breeze. Hearing the unrepentant stalking sounds, the joyful leaps and rolls Suriel made behind him, filled him with a boundless satisfaction and a deep joy.

Once inside the cabin, he found some clothes and started in the kitchen, preparing the steaks to broil and chopping vegetables for a salad.

Suriel hopped on the counter, taking over most of its surface, and pawed at the bread hopefully.

"Carbs aren't good for you, you know," Harry said, chucking him under the chin. Suriel stuck out his barbed tongue and dragged it across Harry's jaw, then his nose, then his cheekbones, until Harry laughed. "Fine, fine—we'll have bread and butter with our steak and salad. You win."

Suriel sat back on his haunches and started cleaning a massive paw in satisfaction, while Harry kept working.

"I know what you're doing, you know." He reached into the tiny refrigerator and pulled out a butter cube, then cut it in half on the cutting board.

Suriel continued to lick his paw blandly while Harry put the other half back.

"You think if you just sit there and be you, but something that can't actually talk back to me, I'll open my heart and sing like a canary. I'm not stupid, you know."

Harry unwrapped the butter cube and started mashing it in a bowl.

Suriel switched to his other paw.

"I just don't know what else you think I have to talk about that you can't contribute to. Books, music, philosophy—we do pretty good at that. But I can't go on and on about the corruption of civil government or the political misinformation made possible by a ceaselessly changing language when you're a cat."

Suriel shot his back leg up and proceeded to lick his genitals, looking up at Harry hopefully while Harry peeled the garlic to go into the butter.

"Put those things away. The cat isn't sexual, mine or yours. It does nothing for me."

Suriel put his leg down and gathered his limbs underneath him, glaring at Harry somewhat indignantly.

"I didn't say *you* weren't sexy," Harry soothed. "I just said...." He puffed out a breath and opened the bag of sourdough bread to pull out a couple of slices each. "See, when we were first turned into cats, it was summat—*fuck*—somewhat of a shock. But that first trip with Emma, where we weren't allowed to change? We all sort of started to realize the freedom we had. Nobody after us, nobody going 'Hello, boy, can you do a thing for me?' And it didn't matter what the thing was either. It could have been suck a cock, it could have been chop wood, or sometimes it was go to school or church and get religion. Fact was, *we didn't care*. 'Hello, boy!' was always something that made the three of us feel like shit and hate the world. So being cats, there was none of that."

Harry sighed and pulled out the cookie sheet from under the stove, then ranged the buttered bread on it to go into the oven when the steaks were done broiling.

Then, everything done and waiting for the meat to finish, he washed his hands and leaned against the counter, arms folded thoughtfully.

"And Leonard and Emma, they knew better. They didn't *make* us do anything, but Edward and I were raised by mothers who taught manners, and we would turn to help them, and Francis hated to be left out, so he'd turn and help too. And we didn't have to turn to learn lessons and spells. We could stay safe and do that, and Emma let us. The cats were safe. All we ever got as cats were pets and mice. All anybody asked of us was affection and to go use the sandbox outside. So sex isn't that. Sex is human. It's what your body does as a human. It means you have to use your hands and your heart and engage them in all sorts of suspicious activities that could get you hurt. So no. I'll fondle your ears and scratch your ass all you want as a cat, but I'm not going to have sex as one."

He started scratching Suriel right behind the ears to punctuate that last thought, and Suriel responded with a purr that rattled the countertop.

"And besides," he added consideringly, "you can't use lubricant if you don't have any thumbs, and do you *know* what your penis does in that form? It's *nasty*. I don't know how lady cats stand it. It's like God tried to punish cats for not giving a shit, it really is."

Suriel turned human and fell off the counter laughing.

"Augh!" Harry's surprise was unfeigned. "There's a naked lunatic laughing on my floor!"

"Oh dear heavens!" Suriel whooped. "Oh my giddy aunt! *Harry!*" He pulled his long legs up to his chin and tried to control himself, and Harry nudged him out of the way.

"Do you mind, Suriel? The meat's ready to turn, and then we can eat in about three minutes."

Suriel rolled to his side and finished his laugh, picking himself up and wiping under his eyes. He stood back while Harry turned and seasoned the steaks, and as soon as the oven was closed, moved forward, wrapping his arms around Harry's waist.

"That was lovely," he purred, nuzzling Harry's ear. "I've not had a laugh like that in millennia of living."

Harry let some of the resentment that had been building ease out of his spine and let his head drift back onto Suriel's shoulder. "What was so funny?" he asked, Suriel's touch making it clear that he was not the butt of a joke.

"That you opened your heart—and it was lovely. It was honest and real, and it gave me a lot of insight into you, Harry. I won't prevaricate. But that look into your deep and beautiful soul was tempered by something very… animal. It's the contrast between the two, you understand? It's made angels laugh for millennia."

Harry laughed softly to himself and turned to take Suriel's mouth. "Laugh all you want," he said between kisses. "Just don't ever leave me out of the joke."

Suriel's mouth on his was heaven, and only the timer, beeping rudely, kept them from burning the steaks.

But Suriel broke off and went to dress while Harry finished with the meal. He came back to eat at the small kitchen table after it had been set. Harry, in a burst of whimsy, lit a single candle and turned off the lights.

Suriel smiled almost shyly as he sat down. "This is marvelous, Harry. What's the occasion?"

Harry turned away and started dishing up salad before passing the bowl. "We are," he mumbled. "Do you think I make love to an angel every day?"

"No." Suriel served himself food and grew suddenly sober. "And I am still dizzy from making love to anyone at all. A celebration is a nice idea."

"It's just...." Harry felt compelled to go on. "It's just that I'm grateful," he said, sawing at his steak. "You... I don't know how it will work exactly. You'll disappear on me one day, leave me alone. But whether I see you or not after that, you're going to go through an ordeal—don't think I don't know that. And I'll be stuck here, waiting, wondering, and you will be in *pain*. Just so you can see me again." Tears. Not painful, just... falling. He could either hide them against his shoulder, or he could look at Suriel with tears in his eyes and acknowledge the hurt between them.

He looked up, met Suriel's warm brown eyes under bright red-gold brows, and smiled. "Would be gentlemanly of me to say thank you. That's all."

Suriel grabbed his hand and kissed it—but he didn't cry. "You're welcome, Harry. I don't know how it will happen either. I was given a finite time down by your side. At the end I could either choose to go back to stay—or to go plead my case." He looked away. "My mind was made up by the first kiss in the swimming hole."

Harry's heart twisted. "It was a very good kiss," he admitted, hoping for Suriel to look back. "I just wish I knew how to help you."

"You helped me make up my mind," Suriel said, granting his wish and looking at him fondly. "But that is all I know, my lover. That no matter what the trial, no matter what the tribulation, it will all be worth it for me to come back." He grimaced. "But you need to promise to be here, Harry. Your past is still out there, and just because you've told me why it scares you doesn't mean it's going away."

Harry cupped his cheek and smiled slightly. "You come back to me, angel, and I'll be waiting for you. Don't worry. It's a promise."

Suriel grinned at him and released his hand so they could go back to eating.

"Harry?" he said with his mouth full.

"Yeah?"

"Do you have any other insights to being cats that I might find amusing?"

Harry grinned and swallowed his steak. "Sure. Rodents. I get that they're a perfect source of protein, and that cats are apex predators to keep the vermin down, but seriously. Has God not heard of legumes? Because sometimes I would just rather not. They crunch. The bones stick in my throat. And when I'm a human, thinking back to what they taste like as a cat, I'd just really rather have Brussels sprouts and broccoli and call it a day."

Suriel guffawed, and the meal—which had grown grave and quiet—finished on a lovely high note.

That evening, after Suriel cleaned up, Harry left the front door open and blew out the candle, and the two of them lay on the bed, side by side, hands burrowing under shirts and shorts as they spoke quietly of people they had known and things they'd like to do someday, in the future, when forever stretched before them like a carpet of clover.

Harry couldn't have said why silence fell or who kissed whom. All he knew was that Suriel rolled him over to his back again, and they wrestled out of their clothes in short order. Suriel's hands, his lips, his skin, all of it slid against Harry's naked body, and he felt protected and real, in a way he didn't think clothes could do.

Suriel kissed down his chin, down his throat, the centerline of his chest. His mouth on Harry's cock was secondary to the heat of his body, the tenderness of his touch. He played until Harry was sobbing for breath, tugging fingers through that glorious satin fall of hair, and then he pulled up and positioned his slickened erection at Harry's opening.

"You like this, Suriel?" Harry taunted softly. "It's a human, animal… ahhhh…."

"I like being a human animal," Suriel whispered in his ear. He pushed slowly, and again, and again, until the rocking, the ebb and thrust of their bodies felt as massive and terrible as waves upon a beach.

Harry's orgasm crested, slow and huge. He dug his heels into Suriel's thighs and clenched his fingers in the muscles of his back. The little groan of completion Suriel made exploded like fireworks in Harry's heart, but it didn't even ripple the sacred hush of the night.

Suriel collapsed to the side, pulling Harry into his embrace, and they caught their breath in the dark while moonlight flooded in through the open door.

"Why don't we make love outside, under the stars?" Suriel asked, tracing runes in the sweat of Harry's chest.

"Because we haven't found a spell yet that will keep the mosquitos away," Harry told him. "Edward spent an entire year trying. All we did was make the marsh flies extra bloodthirsty. It was embarrassing."

"Why aren't they coming in through the door?"

"Emma has a geas on all our thresholds. Nothing that will draw blood or means us harm can pass." Harry yawned. "What are you doing on my chest—and don't say nothing because I can feel the magic burn."

"Protection," Suriel murmured. "I've seen entirely too much of your blood, Harry. I have no idea how long I'll be gone. If I can't come back and fix you, you'd better be damned invincible."

"I'll take the invincible, thank you very much." Harry pulled Suriel's hair back from his eyes so he could see them gleam in the moonlight. "But I'll be plenty damned when you leave, and I shall live there until you come back. Perhaps we can leave that out of the invincibility spell, okay?"

Suriel finished the rune he was working on and moved his fingertips to the contours of Harry's jaw. "You're so wise," he said, his mouth pulled up in a faint smile. "How did you get to be this wise?"

"I've lived two lifetimes—I'd like to hope I've learned something." Harry's heart was sliding into melancholy. "How long will you be gone?"

"A year? A hundred? I have no idea." And then, as though he doubted. "You'll wait for me?"

Harry's laugh held no humor. He turned his head and sucked Suriel's thumb into his mouth so his damned angel would stop casting spells long enough to hear him. "I've waited this long, haven't I?" he demanded upon Suriel's gasp.

"You were not chaste the entire time," Suriel said primly.

"I wasn't falling in love," Harry retorted.

Even the air seemed to stop moving.

"You're in love with me." Suriel's voice held nothing but the deepest satisfaction.

"I've said that already."

"Probably—but I'm savoring the moment. It's joyous."

At once, Harry felt urgency. He scooted up and captured Suriel's mouth. Their blood heated, their movements grew frantic, and this time was rushed, a frantic rutting into each other's hands, a need to hold the other one as long as possible until pleasure exploded for them both.

This time sleep took them while the spend was still cooling on their fingers.

Suriel woke up, sometime near dawn, and snuggled up to Harry's back, pressing his erection between his thighs.

A fumbling for the lubricant, and again.

When they woke up in the morning, Harry was marked by his lover, inside and out, and even Suriel's half-hooded gaze at breakfast was sultry and possessive.

Harry served him pancakes, just to watch him delight in the strawberry preserves Emma had stocked in the refrigerator, and Suriel seemed very happy to indulge in human food some more. But as they were sitting at the table, talking about preserves and how to keep summer in a glass jar to break open again for winter, Suriel turned that hooded, sultry gaze on Harry while he was talking.

Harry licked his lips nervously, and he didn't remember much after that, except Suriel had to bear him up in the shower as they rinsed preserves and whipped cream off their bodies, and his backside was getting sore.

But Suriel kissed his neck in the shower, and his heart sped up and...

And again.

Finally, in the afternoon, Harry chivvied Suriel out the door and into his cat form so he could spend some unmolested minutes talking to his family on the phone. Suriel went, his tail twitching, his whiskers in a dither, and Harry knew he'd better hurry up with his phone call before they ended up in bed.

"Harry!" Edward sounded out of breath and distracted—but not too distracted to give Harry a ration of crap. "You sore yet?"

"Yes, you buggering asshole. What's it to you?"

Edward's deep chuckle of satisfaction was wholly concentrated on Harry's happiness. "You should try topping sometime, Harry. Isn't that how you usually like it?"

Harry groaned. "You are horrible, and I regret everything I ever told you in confidence. How is the search for Anya? Have we found her yet? Do we know what happened?"

"Not good," Edward told him, suddenly serious. "She was targeted by someone who'd been studying her habits. We asked, and Krista was supposed to be at the party too. Emma did some snooping around *Krista's* friends, and it turned out she'd had someone looking into her background too."

"Oh shit. A girl only gets abducted once in her life, right?"

"Unless it's the gift that keeps on giving," Edward agreed grimly. "Yeah, we think this has to do with their first abduction—almost payback for getting away in Vegas."

Harry's heart sank. Too many god-awful things attached to that trip to Vegas. He thought getting nearly beaten to death was the worst part, but hearing Big Cass had been there made that so much more special. That Cass's outfit was back in the lives of the girls who had gotten away—that was bad news indeed.

"So, you didn't happen to ask Krista if she remembered one of her captors, did you?"

"Yeah." Edward's shudder was audible. "She remembers him, Harry. Big and bad and large as life. Now the good news is, if they want to use Anya again, they're going to have to treat her right. She's old enough, she's got to be prettied up before they can sell her, and that will buy her some time. The bad news—"

"Is if they got her for another reason, they've had her for a week." Harry's heart ached in his chest. "Suriel and I can be down there in eight hours," he said. "There's no reason the two of us can't come and help— this is getting urg—"

"No reason?" Edward yelped indignantly. "No reason? You're on your *honeymoon*, man. This could be the closest thing you get to Happy Ever After."

Harry made an injured sound he couldn't quite help. "He's going to get pulled away," he confessed, not sure if Edward had understood this would happen, even under the best-case scenario. "We don't know when. But he'll disappear and I'll just have to wait for him, and in the meantime, we can't call him or know he's out there or—"

"Or if he's coming back," Edward finished for him. "I get it, Harry. Look—Emma told me she's got a boomerang on you—"

"Seriously?" Oh Lord, that took some doing, and it was totally in Emma's wheelhouse. "When does she get good at these things?"

"I swear she practices in her head when she's painting. It's sort of irritating, actually—I could practice for a year and not be as good as she is after a month of getting ready for a show. But she's got a boomerang on you, and if we need you, we'll pull you. Now does that put you at ease?"

Harry thought of it, of the likelihood of getting pulled into a gunfight naked with a full erection, completely concentrating on a whole other activity.

"Not exactly."

Edward guffawed. "Well, maybe put your boxers on while you sleep, and at least you know you'll be covered *then*."

"Has anyone told you that you have a miserable fucking sense of humor?" Harry asked sourly, and Edward laughed again.

"Only you, at least six times a year. Just be aware, okay? We'll call you. But otherwise…." Edward's voice softened. "Take the time, my brother. You love him. There's no sin in celebrating that. Don't talk to me about duty either. You go above and beyond ninety-nine percent of the time. This is a tiny karmic window to feed your soul. It's necessary."

"I just don't—"

"I know you don't. Now shut up and go top. I'm sure he'll love it. Later."

The line clicked dead, and Harry growled and put his phone back on the charger.

Then he turned cat and ran out the door, wondering if Suriel felt like swimming again.

FIGHTING NAKED

TWO DAYS passed. Three. Four.

Harry managed to forget the sword of Damocles hanging over his head, ready to separate him from his lover without notice, and managed to simply enjoy.

They cooked, they talked, they made love. Harry spent the time in a sort of delirium of arousal and ecstasy, and he could never remember how. Not how they made love—he remembered every moment of Suriel's skin sliding over his, of Suriel's body inside him—but how he managed to table his nagging worry for his family, his terror of Big Cass, his vast, aching fear that when Suriel disappeared Harry would be nothing, a fraud, the brittle exoskeleton of a fiercely armored creature.

Those fears he put away in a neat little box, and for those charmed days with Suriel, he was whole, unfettered, unafraid.

He cooked every meal, watched Suriel for his favorites, taking careful notes for Suriel's return. When Suriel found out what he was doing, the sunrise smile on his face made Harry's chest ache.

"What?" he asked, turning the fried chicken breast and keeping his face averted so Suriel couldn't see his flush. "Why that smile?"

"Hope, Harry! You're daring to hope."

Harry busied himself with the other three chicken pieces. "Is that so hard to believe?"

Suriel moved behind him, mindful that Harry was busy with something relatively dangerous.

"No," he whispered, moving his lips along Harry's nape. "It just gives me faith that I'll return. You understand, don't you?"

Harry nodded and turned the last piece of chicken. "If I believe you can do it, you believe," he said dutifully. A child's lesson, perhaps—but he hadn't known it, felt it in his heart until just this moment. He poked

114

at the chicken one more time, decided it was mostly done, and turned off the heat.

Then turned in Suriel's arms and captured his mouth.

"I thought we were going to eat?" Suriel teased as Harry backed him across the kitchen and to the bed.

"That's not what you thought." Harry chuckled, scraping his teeth across Suriel's bare chest.

"No." Suriel hissed in a breath as Harry captured his nipple, throwing his head back and gasping.

"You thought you were going to bugger me raw again."

Suriel sank onto the bed, and Harry fell to his knees before him. With a quick shucking motion, he had the cargo shorts Suriel had been wearing pulled down off his thighs and had taken that lovely fine cock into his mouth, swallowing until he could feel it in the back of his throat.

Suriel bucked, and Harry kept pressure, enjoying Suriel's fingers tugging at his hair. "Are you getting tired of the buggering?" he asked, and Harry tugged gently at his testicles in answer. He slurped his way back and grinned over Suriel's nude body, noticing the wings spread out behind him.

"I am not," he answered, nuzzling the inside of Suriel's thigh. When they'd first made love, he'd been nearly hairless, and what had grown was downy and without color. Now the hair on his legs was pale flame-gold and fine—but definitely masculine, the detail of a mammal coming into his skin.

Harry lowered his head and pulled one newly furred testicle into his mouth and laved it gently before releasing it and moving to the other.

"You know," Suriel breathed, "you could always... ahh... bugger me!"

Harry chuckled and slid his palms from Suriel's backside up to the crook of his knees, spreading his legs. "I thought of that," he murmured, letting his lips and tongue tease the head of his cock. "I did." He parted Suriel's cheeks and licked a straight line down his crease, pausing to breathe on the sensitive pucker of flesh.

"So something is holding you back?"

Harry laughed, goaded by the outraged, frustrated ring of Suriel's voice. "I'm torn," he said before lapping delicately and then tapping with his fingertip. The muscles under his hands thrummed with self-restraint, and Suriel tugged on his hair in desperation. Suriel's entire position, sprawled, wanton, begging for carnality, sent waves of desire pulsing straight to Harry's groin.

"Torn between *what?*" Suriel demanded. Harry answered him with another lick, and Suriel's groan shook the bed. "*Harry!*"

Harry licked a tight buttock. "Torn between wanting to save it, so you have something to come back and learn about being human...." He sucked on his finger, getting it sloppy, and played with Suriel's entrance.

"*And?*" Suriel begged.

"And...." Harry taunted, sucking the head of Suriel's cock into his mouth again and teasing with his tongue while thrusting his finger in slowly and pulling it back.

"*Harry!*" Suriel gasped, hands pounding the bed on either side of him.

Harry pulled back, sucking hard, so Suriel's flesh made a popping sound when it pulled free of Harry's lips. "And getting buggered now," he whispered. "And I'll make love to you so sweet, it'll feel so good, you'll have no choice but to make it back to live by my side."

"That one. Oh please.... Harry, that one!"

Suriel fumbled with the small plastic bottle, and Harry took it, locking his fingers around Suriel's tightly for a moment. He pushed up so they could look each other in the eyes, but he didn't pull his finger from the tight grip of Suriel's body.

"You sure?" he asked, feeling wicked and noble, both great emotions in the same breast.

"Please, Harry." Suriel closed his eyes and arched his back, his whole body aroused beyond endurance by the easiest, simplest penetration. The spasm of arousal passed, and he gazed at Harry with limpid eyes. "I want to take you with me, inside my flesh, like you are in my heart."

Ah, animal needs—they would be Harry's undoing. He pulled from Suriel's body and stripped, using another copious dose of lubricant before positioning himself.

"You ready, then?" he asked, poised too far back to lean over and reassure him with kisses. But this wasn't that kind of lovemaking, was it? This was the gift of possession, and it needed care at the first.

Suriel gazed at him, helpless, vulnerable, needy.

"I have faith in you," he said, a faint smile pulling at the corners of his full, wide mouth. "You give me such pleasure every day... ahhhhh...."

Harry slid inside him, slowly, surely, feeling the resistance, waiting, receding, rocking forward again. Suriel greeted every rock back with a soft cry of protest, every rock forward with a grunt of welcome.

And Suriel's grip around Harry's body—oh! Exquisite. Harry kept thrusting, a clammy sweat breaking out over his back as he thought of hurting Suriel with this act, of even once, even a little, giving Suriel reason to regret what he'd just given to Harry, a lowly mortal who had been in the wrong place at the right time.

Suriel arched his back with acceptance and wrapped his long legs around Harry's thighs. Harry—deeply entrenched in his lover's body now—fell forward, weight on his elbows. Suriel grabbed a pillow and shoved it under his hips, giving them both a better angle.

"Ooooohhh...."

"It's good," Suriel panted. "Sooooo good. I'm full of you, Harry. As full in my body as I've been in my heart. Don't leave me... not now."

"No," Harry whispered, pulling back just enough to thrust forward. "If I'm torn away from you, it's not because I wanted to go."

Suriel groaned as Harry bottomed out. "Not your body, your heart. Never leave me in your heart."

Harry thrust again. "Never."

"Never leave me in your heart."

Oh! Suriel! "As if I could," Harry sobbed, thrusting again.

"Promise, Harry!" Suriel cried. "I'm so scared!"

"Never!" Harry pounded again, heartsore at the admission from his angel. "Always by your side."

"Please!"

"Always!"

"Harry!"

He was scared. Harry leaned forward, keeping their bodies locked together, and kissed him, kissed away his fear, kissed away his desperation. His hips kept moving, their rhythm hard and exacting but not furious. He wanted Suriel raised up, up, up into the realms of pleasure before he came apart.

Suriel arched into the kiss, taking Harry's body into his own, starving with need. There were no words then, only the slap of their bodies, the harshness of their breathing, the whimpers of craving from Suriel's throat.

"Ahh!" Suriel broke away from him, shaking, undone, and Harry pushed up on one arm so he could slide a hand between them and grip Suriel's cock, stroking hard and without mercy. Suriel bucked, crying out, his muscles rippling in completion. Then and only then, as his come scalded over Harry's fist, landing hot and slick between them, did Harry let his vision go white, go dark, red-and-gold fireworks exploding behind his tightly clenched eyes.

His heart thundered so loud in his ears he almost couldn't hear Suriel gasping his name.

But only almost.

"Suriel," he whispered, dragging his lips across Suriel's chin, down his neck, over his shoulder. "Suriel. My brave angel."

"Harry," Suriel whispered back. "Brave Harry. My boy."

"Carry me with you," Harry murmured into his ear. "Carry my seed, my love. Carry all of me with you. While there's breath in my body, I'll always believe in your love."

Even in the shadows of nightfall, Harry could see diamond tracks of helpless tears.

"Do you think less of me?" Suriel asked, gazing at Harry anxiously.

"To know you're afraid?" Harry licked the path of a teardrop, shivering in the joy of the salt. "No."

"No?"

"It makes me know you care about the outcome," Harry told him, giving him a quick kiss. "It makes me know this is important to you. That this is real."

Suriel wrapped his arms tightly around Harry's shoulders then, and Harry allowed himself to collapse, sliding from the sanctuary of Suriel's body in favor of lying on top of him, all the skin touching all the skin.

"We are real. We are the only thing that is real. The place I'm going, the tests I'll be given, you and me, this moment here—this is the real I need to come back to."

Harry managed to chuckle in spite of the ache in his chest, the harsh reminder that these charmed days were not for lasting. "You're sure it's not the chicken?" he teased.

Suriel nodded and smiled. "Although I do have an appetite now."

Harry smiled again and rested his head on Suriel's shoulder. They would eventually get up and make ready to eat, but for now they were hungrier for the reassurance that these days, these moments of heaven in each other's arms, might not have been in vain.

That night, Harry lay in bed trying to memorize the contours of Suriel's face in the moonlight. He lay, replete and sated, eyes closed, mouth parted, a faint smile on his face, while Harry stroked his chest randomly, tired but not wanting to fall asleep, not just yet.

"Do you like what you see?" Suriel murmured, keeping his eyes closed.

"Always."

"What's wrong?"

"You're leaving soon," Harry said baldly. Edward hadn't called that night, hadn't answered his phone call. He was worried on more than one front. "You're leaving, and I've got one thing to do—and I might not be able to do it."

Suriel's eyes snapped open. "What's your one thing? Why can't you do it?"

"Stay alive," Harry said. "And life's uncertain—I can only try."

Suriel nodded gravely. "Try hard," he whispered. "Try with all your heart."

Harry nodded back. "You too."

They kissed then, and Harry thought they would make love, but Suriel pulled him hard into his embrace, and instead they fell asleep, limbs tangled, as much bare skin touching as possible.

119

At dawn, Harry felt the pull in his stomach that meant magic was coming.

"*Suriel!*" he called out, opening his eyes in time to hear Suriel scream. Even as Suriel disappeared, Harry saw the scores of the whip opening the flesh of his arms, his face, his shoulders.

Right before Harry's ears popped brutally, Suriel's body faded into mist.

WHEN HARRY opened his eyes, he was standing naked behind a group of men holding semiautomatic weapons.

In front of them, staring down the barrels of the guns, stood Harry's family. Emma and Leonard clutched hands, Leonard's mouth moving in a sotto voce spell Harry could only imagine. Edward crouched, impressive shoulders flexed, with a blood-dripping machete in either hand, and Francis growled through his human throat, his face battered and angry, his eyes wide and fully blue with the slitted black pupils of a cat.

Emma's lovely face relaxed into a smile as she saw Harry. "We waited as long as we could," she said apologetically.

Slowly, seven sets of eyes turned to see who she was talking to, and seven men threatening deadly force to the people Harry loved most turned bruised, sliced, scratched, and bewildered faces to see what fresh hell had just erupted out of thin air.

"Hello, boys," Harry growled, fury and fear and anguish making him mean. "I see you saved the best for last, didn't you?"

Behind them, Leonard raised his voice in the finale of the spell, and the guns tore themselves out of the men's hands, rocketing through the air in a giant arc, melting and twisting into uselessness as they flew.

Harry laughed, a brutal, angry sound he remembered Big Cass making right before Cass went on a beating spree that left the brothel bruised and bleeding.

With a howl of rage, he jumped into the fray.

CROSSROADS

"STOP!" EDWARD yelled, hauling at Harry's arm. "Stop, Harry—they're down! They're down! If you keep this up, they'll be dead!"

Harry's vision still bled—but then, so did the men at his feet. He raised a bare foot to kick the nearest one in the nose when Edward slapped his face, *hard*.

"Harry! What will Suriel say?"

Harry froze, brain processing, body still set on "kill." "Suriel's gone," he said numbly. "He got called back when I did...." Harry closed his eyes and saw two Suriels—one the haunting, gentle lover he'd gazed upon that night, and the other the frightened, tortured celestial being who had vanished before his eyes. "He's being tortured as we speak."

Edward's hands on his shoulders became an all-encompassing embrace. "Oh, Harry—I'm so sorry. But we need you. All of you. Your mind too. They have Bel, Harry. Big Cass has Bel."

Harry went limp in Edward's arms. "Bel? Oh my God. Bel?" He looked up, a sleepwalker waking from a dream, and glanced around at his surroundings. Dry air sapped the moisture from his skin, the breath from his lungs; and the sun coming up over hills at the far end of the long horizon burned hot and so damned bright. They were at a storage unit warren off the freeway, Harry assumed, but he had no idea which one.

"Where *are* we?" he asked, squinting. "And how in the hell did Big Cass get Bel?"

Francis appeared at Harry's elbow, whimpering disconsolately, and Harry pulled back enough to draw his brother to his chest and accept Edward's hug too. He recalled Suriel's words about Francis and Bel and the change in their relationship over the last year.

121

"We'll get him back," Harry whispered, nuzzling the pale blond hair at Francis's temple. "Don't worry, Francis. I've lost my lover. We won't let you lose yours."

Francis moaned softly and broke into tears, and Harry came fully human to himself and comforted his brother like the child he'd never been allowed to be.

"Edward?" Harry all but begged as Francis wound down on his chest. "Could you...?"

"All we've got is hand-me-downs," Edward apologized, eyeballing the guards Harry had taken out. "Do you see one you'd like?"

"The less blood the better," Harry told him. "That one there, with the basketball shorts, looks like my best bet."

Edward grunted and started pulling off the guy's boots. "Silly thing to wear to illegal activity," he muttered, tugging hard. "*This* is why it pays to put on combat gear." The guy moaned, and he hit the thug in the face with the boot, then threw the boot at Harry. The second came sailing over before he pulled the shorts down the guy's thighs.

"Oh thank God," Harry breathed. He shifted Francis to Leonard for consolation and found he could function in this place, in the non-panic, the non-freaking-out place in his head.

"What?" Edward glanced at him before chucking the shorts.

"He's not going commando!"

Harry snagged the shorts as they smacked against his chest and put them on, then started on the boots, which didn't fit half-bad. Edward worked the tank and the plaid shirt off, and while Francis took deep breaths and got himself under control, Harry finished dressing.

He wrinkled his nose. "This asshole smokes," he muttered. "As soon as we get out of here, this shit's getting burned."

"Yeah, Harry, that's our priority." Edward tried to sound insouciant, but Harry got a look at him—he was worried and angry, his jaw locked, a few terrible bruises healing on his face while he helped Harry get situated.

"Well, it should be," Harry sallied. "I got pulled out of bed, and you didn't let me kill anybody." They needed him. His family needed him. Beltane Youngblood was somehow in Cass's clutches, and that could not stand. Francis was barely human and Edward was coldly furious enough to summon a hurricane, and Harry needed to keep that from happening too.

Francis pulled away from Leonard, his heart-shaped face distorted by a bloodthirsty snarl. "I'll do the killing," he purred, and Harry didn't even need Edward or Leonard to tell him that had to be stopped.

"I'm going to ground you right now if you don't pull back your whiskers, Francis Youngblood. Bel needs you human, and so do we. Now somebody tell me what happened!"

At that moment Emma trotted up to them from the two battered SUVs parked about a hundred yards away. "They left the keys in the ignition," she said happily. "Because they're not that bright and they're destined to die in some mobster's bathroom, drowning in vomit." The air shimmered around her as she spoke, and all the men grimaced.

"Did you see that?" Edward asked rhetorically. Of course they'd seen it. They'd been studying for a century to know exactly what that shimmer meant. "Did you see what our mother just did? Way subtler and crueler than turning them into kibble, Francis. That curse isn't going to just go away, you know."

"That was perfect," Francis said humbly. "Thank you, Emma."

Emma patted his cheek. "He's my son, sweetheart. I would have done the same for any of you. Now come along, boys—we can talk in the car." She frowned. "Dammit. Leonard, be a dear. The leader—next to the one in his underwear—he's got a great roll of cash on him. Can you see it?"

Leonard eyed his wife irritably. "And you want me to...."

She rolled her eyes. "If I *touch* him, I'll negate the curse. I'm not being squeamish, I'm being practical."

Leonard arched sand-colored eyebrows in a rather long, tanned face. He was not handsome, by any stretch of the imagination, but the way he and Emma doted on each other could not be doubted. Of course, that didn't mean they hadn't had their squabbles.

"And the dead possum under the house, was that a curse too?" He wrinkled his nose as he rolled the thug over and rooted through his jeans.

"The dead possum was an unfortunate victim of a storm grate," Emma said, shifting her weight as she lied her ass off. "And it was...."

"Unfortunate," Leonard supplied dryly. He pulled out the wad of cash, his face screwed up in distaste. "They're covered in cocaine and... fluids."

The family groaned, and Emma pulled a small bottle of handwash out of her fanny pack and handed it to him. "It's blessed," she reminded him. "Maybe you can just smear some across the whole bundle. Now come on, boys. I don't think Bel is in immediate danger, but that's only because they think he'll fetch a good price. The minute he gets too troublesome to be useful—"

"Remember, he's been studying too," Leonard said softly, his earlier pique gone. Keeping his hands away from her, he leaned over and kissed her temple. "We'll get our boy back, my darling. In the meantime, let's get going and brief Harry."

"Who showed up in not even his briefs," Edward quipped.

Harry rolled his eyes. "You've been waiting to say that, haven't you?"

Edward looped an arm over his shoulders, and Harry looped his around Francis's. "I warned you. Did I not warn you? I told you to start sleeping in your clothes."

Harry eyed him with brotherly distaste. "You're the one who's done long-term relationships. Were *you* ever forced to say, 'Hang tight while I get dressed so I don't get pulled away naked to take out henchmen with a hard-on'?"

"The henchmen had hard-ons?" Francis asked, giving Harry some hope. "Because they were about to kill us, Harry. That's pretty gross."

Harry got another whiff of the clothes he was wearing and held on to the contents of his stomach. "Those guys were all bad. I don't know what to tell you. Emma's curse was too good for them. Now is anybody going to tell me how this whole *mishegas* went down?"

"Into the car first," Emma muttered tersely, the time for playfulness and relief over for them all. "We've got some miles to cover, and I don't know when you last ate, but we're going to need some fuel for what's to come."

Harry allowed himself to be herded into the foul-smelling SUV— but not before he and Edward did a thorough search for drugs. They found two keys in the door panels, three in the wheel well, and three more duct-taped to the inside of the engine compartment. Edward pulled a hunting knife from a loop on his belt and made short work of gathering the lethal little bundles and dumping them next to the SUV they were leaving behind.

"Should we dispose of them?" Francis asked uncertainly. "Someone could find them driving along—"

"Or the wind could come whipping across the road and blow cocaine for miles," Emma said tartly. "None of us blows lasers out our asses, Francis, and we've got to get a move on!"

"Wait," Edward muttered thoughtfully. He walked toward the pile of drugs and inscribed a pentagram around them, then grabbed twigs off a nearby tumbleweed and lit them on fire with a simple spell, placing a tiny burning taper at each of the five points. Harry watched him, trying to get a bead on the magic he was using, and Edward said, "Any of your knuckles still bleeding?"

Harry grunted no. "But you're welcome to open up a cut," he said. "It can't be yours?"

"No—sorry. Spell caster and sacrifice. It's old magic—before Christ, and damned near before paganism. But here." Harry squatted down beside him and gave his hand over. Edward sliced the side of his wrist, far from a vein but easy to control. The expression he wore struck Harry as remote and unattached as his brother drew his blood and sprinkled it over each of the five burning points. He released Harry's arm and muttered some Latin before pulling what was probably all the moisture in his body into his mouth and hawking a gob of spit into the center.

The flames heightened, tiny explosions of blue heat, and a small bubble formed over the top of the pentagram. The product inside turned brown, and the plastic wrappings over it melted away. What was left when the fire had burned down was a few cups of crumbly, oily residue. The bubble of protection disappeared, and the remnants of a drug run disintegrated softly in the middle. Harry swore and stood, holding his hand out for Edward to take.

125

He looked his brother—his beloved, tart-tongued, practical brother—square in the eye. "Suriel is worried about those spells, Edward. Next time we'll just put it in the gas tank, deal?"

Edward wrinkled his nose. "You hook up with the love of your life and you're suddenly a hundred percent old maiden aunt. Lighten up!" Edward grimaced. "I mean, darken up. We have some people to kill!"

"Yeah, just don't send their souls to Kalamazoo or turn them into frogs or anything, you understand? I'm all for killing anyone who laid a hand on Bel—but this black-arts stuff has got to stop."

Edward gave a grunt and then grabbed Harry's wrist, looking at the cut that would heal normally and not magically. "Well, yeah—it's not like you don't shed enough blood without my help, yeah?"

Harry allowed a small grin to escape. "Nobody ever accused me of that."

THE SUV hadn't been tuned for a while, and the roar of the engine almost precluded conversation. After fifteen minutes of yelling at each other from the front and back seats, Leonard scowled and said, "Fuck this! Wait until we can switch cars!" before nudging Emma to stomp on the gas a little more. "It's going to die in a hundred miles anyway!" he shouted. "We may as well get as much out of it as we can!"

Harry was left in the back seat, sweltering because the air conditioner didn't work and they were apparently driving through hell. Francis sat in the middle, tucked awkwardly behind the seat belt, tail twitching, mouth parted as he panted away his anger and fear, and Edward gazed moodily out the window.

Since everybody's shutting up, Harry prompted him, *tell me what happened.*

Edward glanced at him, arching an eyebrow. *You first.*

Harry shivered and stared outside again. A sign proclaiming they had two hundred miles before entering Las Vegas told him they were on I-15, heading east.

Vegas? He was dismayed but not surprised. It would figure Cass's— or his boss's—base of operations was in Vegas, since that's where Cass had first gotten wind that the three boys he'd let escape more than a century ago were just as alive as he was.

Yeah. We lost Bel in Chula Vista—he saw the truck loading up and changed shape to go investigate. The guards were going to shoot him—

As a dog? Because only the most jaded of bad guys ever went after them in their animal form.

Yes—which tells you all you need to know. Francis shouted his name, they turned, and Bel changed into a goofy college kid, wondering where he was. They loaded him into a truck, and we followed.

What happened to the minivan?

You first. Edward didn't sound like he was in the mood to play around.

What do you want me to say? For the first time since Harry had arrived to the rescue, he let the true import of that morning—coupled with the last few days—sink in.

But Edward surprised him. *I want you to say you were happy.*

Harry's throat swelled, and his next breath was so labored, Francis slid out of the seat belt and rested his chin on Harry's thigh.

"I was happy," he said aloud, stroking Francis between the ears, the way he liked it best.

"Good," Edward said, just loud enough to be heard. *Happy enough to stay?* And because they were mind to mind, without the wind and the engine noise and the general chaos, Harry could hear the pleading in his voice.

I promised him I would. I promised him I'd be stay alive so he could come back to earth and we could live side by side.

Good.

He looked over at his brother and saw Edward wiping his eyes with the back of his hand.

And you, brother?

Edward's mouth flattened. *I am not prepared to accept defeat.*

And then, because Harry wasn't sure if Edward had known either...

Did you know about Bel and Francis?

Edward's eyes widened, and he scratched Francis at the base of his tail. *You little shit,* he said to both of them.

Francis spread his paw pad and began to clean thoroughly, as though he had no idea what on earth Edward could be talking about.

I'm glad for you, Harry said for both their benefits. *But you can't let it get in the way of rescuing him, you understand?*

Francis gazed at him, cross-eyed, not giving away a thing, and Harry flicked his nose.

Don't be bitchy. We love you both.

Francis clawed the back of his hand, drawing it to his chest and kicking out with his back paws, until Harry scooped him up and held him fast against his chest. "Stop it," he said aloud. "This isn't going to change that we know. You're going to have to be human for us, Francis—and that doesn't mean changing in my lap."

It's ours, Francis said clearly in his head. *He's the only thing in my life that's been just mine.*

Harry sighed and rubbed his cheek against Francis's whiskers. *We don't want him that way. We just don't want to lose our brothers.*

Francis went limp in his hold, and Edward reached out and stroked his flank as it drooped over Harry's body. *I've got my own demon lover, Francis. You're welcome to a Labrador retriever, no worries.*

Harry half laughed and rubbed his cheek against Francis's again for good measure. *So*, he said deliberately. *Are we going to tell me about the minivan?*

Edward glared at Emma, who was driving like the SUV had offended her and she was trying to kill it.

"No," he said out loud. "In fact, I don't want to think about the minivan ever again!"

Emma grimaced apologetically. "I'm so sorry!" she called.

Edward shook his head grimly. *Six brand-new soccer chairs in the back, and a carefully accrued shipment of chemical compounds I'll have to assemble from scratch.*

More dark magic? Harry asked apprehensively.

They're what she used to get Leonard out of hell.

Harry took a deep breath and met his brother's eyes. *Really?*

We saved you, Harry. It's time to save Mullins.

Harry smiled at him, eyes burning, absurdly happy. "Oh."

"Oh what?"

"Now I know why you all tried so hard to save me."

Edward and Francis were both staring at him anxiously, almost begging him to say it.

You love me as much as I love you. I never really thought of it before.

And that quickly, he was holding Francis as a person, sobbing in his arms, while Edward draped himself on top of them both in comfort.

THE SUV blew a rod while passing a tiny nameless town. Emma steered it, knocking so loud the pistons sounded like they were coming through the hood, into the one gas station/minimart combo in the place and slumped in the front seat, sighing.

"What now?" Harry asked from the back seat, although neither Leonard nor Emma looked terribly unhappy.

"Now?" Emma glanced back with a weary smile. "Now we go inside and get something cool to drink."

"Cool?" Francis stammered. "Cool? We're... the car.... *Bel!*"

"Is fine for now," she said with determined calm it was clear she didn't feel. A faint smile tugged at her pretty features. "Boys... boys, boys. Please—when Edward and Harry first proposed helping young Mary Quinn escape, do you have any idea how frightened I was?"

Edward pulled his chin in, like he did when he was surprised. "Why would you be frightened? We had a plan, the three of us were clearly superior fighters. We weren't as powerful as we are now, but we had the tactical edge—"

Emma's sudden laugh felt like clear water in that stifling, stinking car. "You did indeed. And I had to trust in the fates, didn't I? Have faith in the God and Goddess, and a little bit in fate, that my three boys would take on this challenge and be all right. Don't you agree?"

Francis hissed like a cat and turned his face to the open window. Next to them, a pickup truck pulled up, one of the bigger models, with primered quarter panels and a smoothly running engine.

"Yes," Harry said, to finish conversation so they could get out of the car. "So you had faith. How is faith going to get us a car?"

Next to the pickup truck, a brown Cadillac pulled up, with a reasonably clean body and a couple of minor dents.

Harry squinted as a tall man with dark curly hair and a cynical twist to his lip got out of the pickup truck, and an older, thinner man with a good-ol'-boy smile got out of the Caddy. They said a few words, the younger guy shrugged, and then he walked around the truck to open the door for his passenger.

"It just will," Emma said insouciantly. "I can't even tell you how I know. Sometimes magic is just trusting the pull under your breastbo—"

Harry got out of the SUV to get a better look at the guy who'd gotten out of the passenger seat of the truck.

"Who are you?" he asked point-blank.

The driver—the dark-haired, cynical one—tilted his head. "You can see him?"

Harry opened his mouth and closed it again, and his friend with the Caddy joined them. "He can see who, Tucker?"

Tucker gave a little gasp and rubbed under his breastbone. "Angel. He can see Angel. And it's them." His smile lost its cynical edge, and he looked at the person he'd let out of the truck. "Angel—this is the reason for the pull."

Angel smiled at them all and waved, and Harry caught his breath.

"You're...." Amorphous was the first word he thought of. Harry couldn't get a lock on Angel's features. He seemed to see a beautiful redheaded woman one moment and a good-looking young man with auburn hair the next. A slim-hipped brunette one moment, a blond lumberjack the next. But even that was superseded by the one familiar and consistent thing on Angel's body.

"Wings," Harry said, awed.

"I don't see them," Edward said skeptically at his side.

"That's because you've never touched them." Harry remembered the feeling of them *not* touching his skin, the whisper-soft presence of something that would never actually make contact but whose beauty could be felt across space and time.

Angel's features resolved themselves into an auburn-haired young man who smiled happily at the Youngblood family. "Look, Tucker. They're all together. Do you want to adopt them too, like Josh's family?"

The older man next to them rolled his eyes. "Are these the people who need the Caddy?" he asked sourly. "We traveled an awful long goddamned ways to just abandon a car with strangers."

Tucker smiled and let his shoulders sag. "Yeah. Give them the keys."

Harry's eyes opened wide as Josh handed Emma the keys in his hand, held together on a key ring with a map of Sacramento on it. "There wouldn't be any clothes in the back of that car, would there?" he asked, his stomach a little fluttery.

Josh said, "Oh damn! I almost forgot, the wife packed me a...." He looked Harry up and down. "Spare change of clothes that I will never see again," he muttered. "Jesus, kid, your life makes me crazy. Can we get a frozen burrito and go home now?"

"I'll come with you," Leonard said, holding out his hand. "Leonard Youngblood. Pleased to meet you."

"Josh Greenaway. And leave me out of whatever you all are doing. Tucker and his damned pulls under his stomach. I'm over it."

"Excellent!" Leonard said, in good humor as always. "Frozen burritos on me!"

Edward and Francis shook hands with Tucker awkwardly, and Emma shepherded them away after giving Harry the keys.

Harry stared at Angel longingly, not able to put a damned thing in his heart into words.

Then Angel saved his life. "He's okay, you know," he said conspiratorially.

"Who is?" Harry rasped—but he was almost afraid to think it.

"Why, the angel you're afraid for. He'll be okay. Have a little faith, can we?"

"It's not always as easy as that," Tucker said gently at Angel's side. He cupped Angel's elbow in a way that bespoke great intimacy.

Angel's wings fluttered, and Harry looked at them longingly. He closed his eyes, remembered Suriel asleep in the night, at peace, ready for what was to come.

131

"I can have faith," he said humbly.

When he opened his eyes, Angel was smiling benevolently at him. Tucker held out his hand. "Good luck to you," he said softly.

Harry took his hand and shook. "Thank you. I'm not sure how you knew, or even what you're doing here—but I'm grateful."

Tucker rolled his eyes. "Don't be too grateful. If I know Josh at *all*, he brought the jeans with no ass, and the T-shirt's gonna say something that will get you beat up in any redneck bar in the country."

Harry laughed. He had to. "They'd have a fight on their hands," he said mildly.

"Oh Jesus—one of *those*. Well, you want to pay it back to me, enforcer, come fight ghosts in the foothills, okay? Those fuckers almost killed me last time."

Angel turned a bleak look toward Harry. "It's important that doesn't happen," he said with so much sincerity Harry found himself nodding too.

"C'mon, Angel. I want a soda the size of Lake Folsom, and more chocolate than should be allowed by law."

They disappeared into the store, and Harry could hear Angel's plaintive "But why would chocolate become illegal?" before the door closed.

He closed his eyes on the blazing asphalt in front of the random quickie mart where their hastily stolen car had died.

Fate. Karma. God or Goddess, *somebody* needed to be thanked.

When his heart felt clear again, he ran to fetch the clothes in the back of the Caddy so he could change in the bathroom. He *really* wanted to get out of these stinking basketball shorts.

ONE SPLASH of water on his pits later, he was taking a giant bottle of water from Leonard and loading into the Cadillac with his family. The vehicle was decently maintained, with leather upholstery and air-conditioning that could probably start icicles on the windows if they ran it long and hard enough.

Harry filled his palm with a handful of M&M's before finally asking Emma what in the hell all that was about.

Since Leonard was driving, Emma could turn around and face him in the back seat. "Do you ever wonder," she began, using her fingertips to smooth his hair back from his temples like she had when he'd been younger. "Do you ever wonder at the odds of three boys being hidden under a bramble bush by the river, just when I needed three boys to hold my power the most? Just when Leonard and I needed a family to care for so we wouldn't be afraid? When Mullins needed a reason to fight his way free of hell and Suriel needed to find his faith again?"

Harry blinked at her. In all this time, he hadn't wondered once. "Should I have?"

"Yes and no," she said, looking supremely catlike—which was funny, because shape-changing was not one of her talents, not anymore. She'd given her cat to her boys, and apparently Leonard had given his dog to Bel so he wouldn't be left out.

"Yes, because…."

"Because curiosity didn't kill the cat—it got him out of trouble when dumb luck wouldn't do," she said practically. "This is something Edward knows, but you and Francis not so much. You'll learn."

Edward made a smug sound next to him, and Francis cuffed him over the head. "So, why no? And Francis, you ass, that hurt."

Francis hissed and turned back to Emma with a bored expression on his face.

He is not okay, Edward thought grimly at Harry.

You think?

"No," Emma continued. She reached across Harry and flicked Francis on the forehead without skipping a beat. "Because it's like being in the eye of a hurricane. When you're on the outside of it, you can see all the mighty forces of the universe that went into creating that one perfect center. During the moment in time that brought us all together, we were in the center. We didn't see the forces that worked around us."

Harry blinked, remembering that moment of calm, watching Suriel sleep, both of them aware that the world was moving but oblivious to the terrible winds in action right at that moment. "Is there ever a time when we're the wind?" he asked wistfully.

Emma smiled and patted his cheek. "Of course, darling. Every rescue we've ever made—those girls were the center. And then we were the wind."

"So what does this have to do with two friends and an angel at the crossroads?" Edward asked sharply. "And you filled this thing up—will it get us to Vegas?"

"As long as we don't stop for hookers," Leonard deadpanned. Emma flicked *him* on the ear, and he grabbed her hand and kissed it before putting both hands on the wheel again.

Emma rolled her eyes but kept talking. "You answered your own question, Edward. Crossroads can be magical places—and the people drawn to them just as magical as we are. I'll wager the men and the angel have been at the center of the crossroads a time or two and have fixed things for people and sent them on their way." She chewed her lip and smiled faintly. "And I'd go one step further. I'm sure there are lots of people out there who could have met us at that exact point, with a car and a clean pair of jeans and a...." She read Harry's T-shirt and winced. "A *Dump Trump* T-shirt. But only *these* guys would bring someone who would...." Abruptly the strength and the optimism faded, to be replaced by the worry Harry had felt gnawing in his stomach since he'd faded from the cabin in Mendocino. "Someone who would give you hope. They *did* give you hope, didn't they, Harry?"

Harry nodded, pulling up a smile to help her have strength when his faded.

"So essentially, they showed up for no other purpose but to have the car we needed and the clothes too," Harry said, seeing the hint of the grand plan again. Emma had been trying to teach them about the forces that drove the world since that first train ride at her knee—but Emma's mind worked that way so naturally, the higher purpose of things sometimes left pragmatists like Harry and Edward in the dust.

"They did indeed," Emma said, turning back around in her seat. "But that doesn't mean we can't be grateful for their service."

Harry gave her a few moments. For one thing, he knew looking backward made her motion sick. For another, he wanted to wait until his heartbeat had calmed down and the sweat had stopped beading on his back and under his neck. When he felt like he could think again, he asked, "How do we know it was Big Cass?"

Emma took a deep breath. "Leonard, I'll let you take that one."

Leonard kept his eyes on the road and took a big pull of his soda before answering.

"Okay, so we started calling the girls who had been rescued in Vegas, and they—to a one—had reported being followed or had disappeared. The girls who *hadn't* disappeared had seen him. And, oddly enough, they *all* had seen him, and they *all* had fought back. One girl called to him—'Hey, motherfucker!'—from her second-story apartment building and dumped boiling water on him, which really, should have just pissed him off. But—and these are her words, mind you—she said it seemed to make him smaller. Another girl just ran at him, attacking, fingernails to the eyes, balls-out. She said he flailed and clocked her across the jaw, leaving her pretty helpless—and then he ran away. So the fighting back really seems to work, especially when it shouldn't. It's got to be him—he's made stronger by fear. I mean, a lot of bullies or abusers are made stronger by fear, but this seems to be in an actual, physical way."

Harry let out a breath. "Tough girls," he said. Tougher than he was—the irony wasn't lost on him either. He'd been the one to rescue them.

"Well, yes, but most of them said they remembered your bravery, Harry, so don't forget that. But anyway, the last girl who was taken lived in San Diego, and we got there mere hours after she'd been dragged away—kicking and screaming, I might add—but not by Cass. So we were close enough to do a scry, and that's when...." He scowled. "Goddammit, Beltane. 'Don't worry, Dad, I'm just going to take a look around. Nobody shoots dogs, right?'"

"Jerk," Francis muttered. Harry was pretty sure he wasn't talking about Leonard.

"So do we have any idea where we're going?" Harry asked, patting Francis on the shoulder. "Or do we just figure Vegas?"

"Well, we figure Cass is probably working for the same outfit we busted a few years ago. We contacted Corbin—you remember him?"

"Bureau for Missing and Exploited Children?" Because they'd cultivated as many contacts as they could in government agencies. For all their resistance to bureaucracy and authority, the Youngblood family was who those people called when things went wrong.

"That's the one. Anyway, he says a guy who looks a lot like Big Cass's boss has a semipermanent thing in Vegas. They have a line on abandoned casinos in the outer parts of the city proper. Every time Corbin gets close to them in one venue, they pick up stakes and move. But they don't have the resources we do. We figure—"

"Put three cats on the ground, see if we get close enough for Francis to hear Bel, and we can do what we need to." Beltane hadn't studied enough, hadn't *practiced* enough to float around in everybody's head the way the familiars could—but he and Francis had been practically in each other's pockets since Bel was born.

"Yes, and I can talk to the birds," Emma added. When she'd shifted much of her power to the familiars in that first act of magic, bird speech had been one of her favorite things to remain in her control. One of the first things the boys had learned was *not* to chase after the birds she spoke to—they were always friends.

Harry had to laugh. "So essentially, we get there and kick a little ass."

"Yup," Leonard said. "Maybe take some names." He smiled, the kind of smile that reminded them all that he'd spent over three hundred years as a demon in hell. "Maybe leave a few bones to be scoured by the desert, unlamented and unlabeled."

Emma smacked his arm. "Leonard!"

But Leonard's fierceness reassured Harry. He tilted his head back into the space between the window and the seat and closed his eyes.

"Wake me when the ass-kicking starts," he mumbled. Edward leaned against him on the left, and Francis leaned against him on the right, the way they'd always leaned, even when they were kids sleeping on their pallet in the brothel. Harry was their center. He'd keep them safe.

And now, now that everything and nothing had changed, he realized he prized that identity. No wonder he'd denied his fear of Big Cass. He would have done anything, pretended anything, faced anything, to be the man his brothers leaned on.

Well, after a hundred and forty years, he was going to have to earn that.

Sleeping now was purely practical—Harry was going to need his strength.

DISSIPATION

FOR ONE reason or another, the Youngbloods had never really embraced Vegas.

None of them liked the lights—perhaps because they'd been born during a different, quieter time, and although they enjoyed technology, they didn't worship it.

The boys had grown up in a brothel. Sex for sale held no appeal. Gambling reminded them of violent days. The crowds felt cruel and impersonal.

The one thing—the only thing—Harry and, as far as he could tell, his entire family appreciated about Vegas was the view of it as they approached from the west, with great clouds overhead as the city rested, small and delineated, on the surface of the great desert.

It humbled him, gave him a moment of pause that he was but a servant to the greater world, and the greater world owed him no favors.

Like Emma's analogy of the tornado or the hurricane, he knew what it was to be but a gust of wind, and mankind was the center.

For Bel's sake, he hoped to be the strongest gale he could summon.

"I hate this view," Edward said, not moving from his lean against Harry's chest. "Makes me feel small."

"And yet you always look," Harry chided.

"Doesn't mean it's not beautiful. Just means…." He took a painful breath.

"We're the best to do what we do," Harry told him, although Edward had probably had this thought as often as Harry. "We know what it means to be small, to have no options, to risk death to get away."

"And then we grew," Edward supplied. He looked to Harry's other side for Francis and found a fluffy, small-boned bundle of denial on Harry's lap instead. "Some of us."

Harry checked very carefully to see if Francis was still awake.

"Did you know?" he asked softly.

"Know what?"

"That they were...." Harry wasn't used to dramatic gestures—he was giving himself a headache trying to do something meaningful with his eyebrows.

Edward looked at Francis and back to Harry. "Francis and Bel?" he asked, making sure.

"Yes!"

"No! Not until now! How did you know?"

"Suriel told me."

Edward snorted. "I had no idea he was a voyeur."

Harry didn't laugh. "We're... I mean, all of us, we're his contact with humanity, I think. He looks... looked in on all of us."

Edward hmmed.

"What?"

"I'll just miss that about him, is all. But I won't mind so much if he's going to be here, a part of us, in our family."

Harry stared at him, struggling for words, and Edward sat up and started rubbing the sleep out of his eyes. "Past the strip, Leonard," he called. "Keep going east." He looked at Harry irritably. "What is your problem?"

"You just assume he's going to make it," Harry said, finally putting his finger on what had blown him away. "You just—"

Edward smiled, not his cold smile or his fierce smile, and Harry remembered why he'd had to work so hard to distract the miners from going after Edward. Edward was the pretty one.

"He brought my brother back to us," Edward said simply. "He can do anything." He frowned at Francis. "Well, almost anything. Those two are going to be a handful, because I'm telling you right now, Emma is dead set on Bel going to Oxford."

Harry managed a nod. Edward's casual assumption that they would get through this—Suriel, Bel, all of them—gave him heart.

"Toward the Air Force base?" Leonard called. "Out by the speedway?"

"Turn before then," Edward said. "Go north on I-95 and take Corn Creek Road. There's not much out there, but you'll see the abandoned casinos before we hit Landy." He glared at Harry. "Which is where we found Harry, right out in the middle of nowhere, not even a road to be found."

Harry shuddered. "I had a bag on my head," he said apologetically. "And by the time you all found me—"

"You needed fluids and bedrest," Edward said shortly. "We know. But I remember. Keep driving, Leonard. We're getting there."

And for Edward, that was a pep talk. Harry realized that more would have scared him and started running his trickier spells through his head, imagining himself as a pen of fire, inscribing the words on the core of his consciousness, to make the words all true.

When Harry looked at this area on a satellite map, he saw some suburban roads, many of them partially completed. Yes, there were state parks and a reservation nearby—but some of the area was flat-out desolation.

And this time of year, it could be hellishly hot.

Still, when they spotted the dusty line of old casinos with the warehouses behind them off in the distance, Harry didn't feel any lifting of the heart. For one thing, this area had been built up with the hopes of becoming a second strip. The optimism had been ill founded. The five casinos had opulent outsides, but only one of them had appointments or even carpeting inside. They'd been built in the sixties and had sat in neglect since, rotting until someone had come along to develop the land into the suburbs that were gradually spreading across the plain. There was a good fifteen minutes of freeway before that happened—and the result was man-made buildings that didn't belong there.

Which would make stopping in front of them look really suspicious.

"Leonard!" Harry said urgently. "Is there any way we can get out of the car without you slowing down? The three of us—"

"We're going too!" Emma snapped. "I know you three think you're the superheroes here, but Leonard and I—"

"I'm not trying to leave you out!" Harry protested. "I'm just saying there's hardly a soul on the highway today. If we slow down and park anywhere near those buildings, we're going to be seen!"

"Well then," Emma returned briskly, "we'll just have to make sure there's nobody left to chase us when we're done, won't we?"

Harry blinked at her.

Well, yes. Emma had been kind and compassionate and strong as long as he'd known her, and that's what Harry tended to remember. What he'd forgotten was that this woman had the audacity to summon an angel and a demon for study long before she'd ever created three tomcats and adopted them as sons.

There had to be a core of fierceness in Emma Youngblood, or she never would have lived this long in the life she'd created for herself.

"Okay, then." Harry smiled his warrior's smile, the one he used when he was spoiling for a fight and proud to do it.

Leonard followed the highway to the turnout, and the air inside the car shifted, shimmered with tension, glittered with the potential for violence and dark deeds.

Harry closed his eyes and began to visualize his enemy in agonizing detail.

He remembered the coarse black jungle of Cass's beard, the flakes of dandruff in his pubic hair, the yellow of his teeth as he laughed, right before fucking Harry until he bled.

He remembered the pain, the constant fear, the dull ache of knowledge that Harry's body—his fragile adolescent body—was rotting from the inside out, and Cass had planted the rot that was eating him alive.

He could recall, in delicate ink lines, Edward's look of disgust and pain as Cass had taken him that first time, while Harry lay practically dying beside him. The way Francis had hidden, a shadow with haunted blue eyes, at the creak of Cass's leather boots on the rough boards of the brothel floor.

He heard the screams of the girls Cass bedded, saw their weary smiles in the morning, washed the bloodied sheets.

Let the fear and the hopelessness wash through him, as it had when he'd been not more than a child.

Then, very deliberately, he remembered that first night with Emma. Remembered Suriel's hands on him, his kindness.

Remembered Suriel's righteous fury as he'd killed Cass the first time, scattering his flesh across the clearing like ashes.

And the memories continued—Harry's first boy after the brothel, his realization that touching another person's skin in intimacy could hold sweetness. Watching Francis practicing his letters one day, in a rare moment as a human, and the wonder on his face as he spelled his own name. Visiting Edward's lovers in their homes, eating dinner with them, the simple kindness of human beings. Doing for John what had been done for him—helping him grow, helping him find a life, watching him forge a family, even if it included no lover.

Harry felt each memory slide into place like a counting bead on a steel string—each one adding strength, flexibility, substance to the person Harry had been when he'd first run through that clearing, terrified and dying, doing his best to pull the only two family he had to safety.

The raw materials of Harry had been there, but every person he'd loved, every person he'd helped, every battle he'd fought and every peace he'd celebrated had created someone stronger, smarter, more able to deal with the terror of his childhood.

And finally, as Harry was feeling his strength in his bones and the ends of his fingertips, he allowed himself to think of Emma and Leonard and Bel.

The look of trepidation on Emma's face as she'd told the boys she and Leonard wanted to have a child, and how they would lose some of their power if they gave Bel the same gifts they'd enjoyed.

"Only so much raw power in the world, my loves. We would have to be willing to share, and then make up the lack with extra study, extra practice, you understand?"

And Harry's heart had swelled with pride, because this was his chance to give back the gifts he'd been given, his chance to love as he'd been loved, his chance to show Emma and Leonard that the family they'd given him was so much more than the ability to spend half his life as a black tom cat.

And once he'd held Bel in his arms, his tiny brother, he'd learned love all over again.

The car stopped, and Harry opened his eyes. Leonard had pulled behind the first casino warehouse, and Harry squinted at them, trying to figure out where Bel was being held.

"The far one," Leonard said quietly. "There's a bunch of cars parked out front. Now what we were thinking was, you three would do recon, and Emma and I will be crouching there in the shade, waiting for your—"

The slam of the car door interrupted him, and Edward cried, "Oh dammit, Francis!"

Harry scooted across the seat, opened the door into the searing Nevada sun, and turned into a fifteen-pound cat, flickering over the sandy asphalt to keep the heat from scorching his paws. Edward ghosted behind them, swearing the whole way.

Goddammit, couldn't wait one lousy fucking moment, could he? Francis, you asshole, Bel's not going to be happy if you get killed! Remember we don't have angel backup this run!

Francis's voice was as delicate as china in their heads.

I don't want to die. I just want to get him back!

I never wanted to die either! Harry barked at him. *Now be careful and wait for us!*

His urgency must have seeped through, because when they flitted to the corner of the last warehouse, Francis crouched next to the beige aluminum wall, tail swishing angrily.

Do we have a way inside? Edward asked.

Harry peered around the corner. The front of the warehouse sported a large loading door that was locked and a smaller standard door—with a cheap door handle. One good yank would open it, Harry estimated, but he couldn't do it as a cat.

He turned human, trying not to groan when the sun hit his exposed skin. That was one thing cats had over people right there—all-over SPF. Very boldly, as though he belonged there, he strode up to the door and yanked on the handle. The door was locked but not shut completely, and it opened with a squeal and a protest of swollen metal moldings against the frame.

Edward didn't have to say a damned thing—Harry could hear his unamused silence.

Did you *bring the WD-40?*

Francis snickered in their heads, and Edward rolled his eyes. For a moment, Harry was reassured. Francis *wasn't* a feral cat—not anymore. Slowly, year by year, he'd become more human.

For Bel, he could keep himself.

Harry held the door, and his brothers flickered in, and then Harry turned cat again and flickered after them.

They had entered a small office, one probably intended for inventory and shipping invoices, but that had never been finished. The windows that would have normally separated it from the rest of the space had never been installed, and the three familiars leaped over the waist-high partition as though it didn't exist.

The warehouse seemed bigger inside than out—but part of that was the almost total darkness everywhere but under the high windows. In the far corner, under the squares of light thrown down by the bitter sun, a group of people huddled, surrounded by hired muscle on camp stools, semiautomatics resting easily against their thighs.

Edward? Could you?

Edward's sleep spells were the best. Harry barely heard him whisper under his breath, and the bored, irritated aura that had surrounded the guards as they'd walked in faded. In its place fell a heavy, soporific stillness—a circus could have rollicked through the warehouse at that moment, and the men slumping on the camp stools would not have so much as dreamed of elephants. Unfortunately, the regular guards weren't all they had to worry about.

Big Cass leaned against the warehouse wall, arms folded as he questioned the people sitting or lying on the cement floor in front of them.

"So," he snarled, spitting on the floor near his feet. "I'll say this one more time. You all should have been used up by now. Who stole that lot of you right out from under Roy Berta's nose?"

The group of women—and one man—stared back up at him impassively, and Harry recognized the girls from the run in Vegas, grown up now, looking capable and angry.

But not scared.

They'd done that, Harry realized. He and his brothers—*they'd* given them the hope to stare down a vicious psychopath with a gun.

"We escaped on our own," said one of the women. Anya—Harry remembered her. Skin the color of pale maple, with almond-shaped green eyes and a pointed chin, her blooming prettiness had been tattered but not destroyed by exhaustion and bruising along the side of her face. "And you were so insecure you had to hunt us down again? That's just sad."

Cass took two steps forward, swinging the butt of his gun at Anya's battered face.

Bel's hand, broad and masculine, blocked the swing, and as Harry and the others dug their front paws in to fly across the dusty floor, he disarmed his captor in one magic-enhanced yank.

"I said don't hit her again," Bel snapped, fitting the weapon against his forearm with the ease of someone who had trained with a father who had utmost respect for weapons. Bel aimed the gun at Cass like he didn't fear repercussions if he shot.

Cass laughed.

"That didn't come out well for you last time you tried it, did it?"

Bel shrugged. "You act like this power is something you earned. It was an accidental gift—those can be taken back."

Cass stared at him. "What do you mean, 'accidental'? The fucker who scattered me across the goddamned wilderness certainly meant to do it!"

Bel rolled his eyes, and his voice took on the patient, slightly pedantic tones of Leonard when he was in the middle of teaching the boys a particularly difficult lesson.

"Yes—the death was on purpose. The resurrection was a byproduct of certain related things." He nodded, and as Harry slunk closer, hugging the shadows, he could see that Bel hadn't remained completely unscathed—he too sported bruises across his face, including a split lip and a broken nose. But then, the wall behind

Big Cass was sprayed with blood, as though a bucket of it had been thrown from ten feet away. Apparently *neither* of them had escaped unscathed.

"Certain related things?" Cass scoffed. *"Certain related things?* I'm *immortal,* cupcake! You saw my blood and bones scattered to the four winds and resurrected before your eyes! Is that going to go *away?"*

Bel huffed, his finger steady on the trigger. "What you fail to realize here is that you're incidental," he said shortly. "Yes, great. You get killed violently and resurrected again and again and again. Immortal fear has given you the power of immortality. But have you benefited from this change? Have you ever, once, thought of using your next life in another way? You continue to be a mindless, violent brute. When you are dead forever, another mindless, violent brute will take your place—nobody will miss you. Nobody will care. And *you* did that. *You* made yourself nothing in the universe. You haven't earned your immortality. You haven't used it to redeem yourself. You're a cipher who can bleed. The minute we cease to fear you, any power, any uniqueness you had in the world—that's gone."

Cass gaped at him—and, oh dear heavens, he shrank. The great brooding, hulking presence of rape and bloodshed grew smaller. Grew less. Became almost nil.

Harry's breath caught in his throat. Oh, dear Bel, who had never had cause to fear in his life—bless him, bless him a thousand times over for learning the lesson of fearlessness at the knees of a man who once used fear as a weapon.

But one man alone—even one as bright and shining as Beltane Youngblood—couldn't conquer the mass of fear that a hundred and forty years of violence and violation had created.

Big Cass started laughing, an evil, angry sound, and his silhouette grew larger and darker with every cackle.

Bel didn't flinch, but Harry couldn't watch anymore.

Edward, Francis, get ready to lead the girls out under the fog.

Wha—? No! I hate this fucking spell! Edward's ginger tomcat glowered angrily, but the light-boned Siamese gave a feline smile.

Can Bel be a dog? There was a certain wistfulness in his voice, and Harry thought he'd been very self-controlled.

If he thinks the girls will follow him. After all, the girls had apparently seen Big Cass get destroyed and reconstitute himself. He was pretty sure the man in their midst turning into a big dog wasn't going to be any stranger.

Francis's affirmative sounded like the chiming of silver bells. Harry watched fondly as their youngest brother whispered between the sitting, watchful women, head-butting them unobtrusively until they petted him so he could give them comfort.

It occurred to Harry how much true good Francis did in this form. While Harry and Edward worked on plans and strategy, Francis worked on calming down the people they were working for, on giving them hope and kindness.

Francis was a lesson right there, in how making victims remember they were human also made them remember how not to be victims.

Slowly—without even realizing it himself, probably—Big Cass's looming, eight-foot shadow of terror shrunk to man size again just as Francis wound himself around Bel's ankles.

Bel shifted his stance but kept the gun trained on Cass. "You're shrinking again," he said pleasantly.

Big Cass grinned unpleasantly, revealing black gaps where teeth should be. "I can fix that," he growled. "Same way I got big in the first place." He reached down to the girl closest to him, who cringed away with an unconscious gasp. "C'mon, sweetheart—you and me. I'll teach you bitches how big I can be!"

Harry had just enough time to wonder—how could he have been afraid of this? Through two lifetimes, Cass had been the bogeyman of his dreams, but he was so small! He'd had the same two lifetimes Harry'd had, but all he'd learned was that death didn't last.

Harry had figured *that* out his first night in the glade, when he'd been bathed in a shower of light and turned into a tomcat.

Just that much crossed Harry's mind, nothing more, when Bel squeezed the trigger and Big Cass vaporized, flying apart in a rain of carnage.

The guards didn't move, but even as Harry and the others watched, horrified, gobbets of flesh and slivers of bone that used to be Big Cass began to flow, migrate, crawl, and fly, coalescing in the center of the blood-spattered wall.

Harry wouldn't get a better chance.

"Bel! Heel!" he called, and his little brother glared at him before morphing smoothly into the giant yellow Lab who had spent hours chasing rabbits among the ferns and redwoods of Mendocino.

And just like Mendocino, where the air smelled of salt spray and skunkweed, the fog began to roll in.

Edward—ever the boys' public face—changed smoothly into a man again and urged the captives, "Drop to your hands and knees and head for the entrance. There's a car toward the back—but move, move, move!"

And still, the fog kept rolling in.

By the time Big Cass had taken on a hulking, man-size silhouette against the back wall, most of the girls were at the halfway point across the warehouse floor.

And the fog was almost too thick to see anything, even his shadow.

Edward, Francis—make sure none of the girls fall behind.

What are you going to do? Edward's voice had the ring of narrow-eyed suspicion in it, but Harry couldn't help that.

Going to make sure he stays dead, Harry replied grimly. *Now get Bel out of here!*

Fine, but we're coming back!

Whatever. Harry trotted, a solid, no-nonsense black cat, low against the floor while he listened to Cass reorient himself to a cloudy, uncertain world.

"Where'd you go, you bloody cowards! And...." A less than delicate sniffing followed. "Where did the fucking cats come from?"

Changing was risky—especially when Harry was still concentrating on the pen of fire in the back of his mind, writing about fog and little cat feet—but he did it anyway.

"Remember me?" he snarled.

Cass squinted through the quickly gathering mist.

"You?" he asked in disbelief. "*You?* I thought it was you—but you were such a sniveling little puke bucket. How in all hells did you make it this far?"

The fear threatened to overwhelm him, as it always had, but Harry made himself laugh anyway, driving it back.

"Don't you get it? I *made* you!" he cried. "I *feared* you. And you came back, again and again, because of that fear!"

"Well, thank you." Cass leered, taking a step forward. "Feel free to fear me some more!"

Harry's stomach cramped, and he longed so hard for Suriel, he almost cried. "No," he replied, voice choked. "You're not real fear anymore. I know what it's like to lose someone—to fear you'll never see them again. Fearing you, when I can do something about you? It's not worth my time."

"It's not worth your—"

Cass ran toward him, sputtering, and Harry regained his little cat feet again and allowed himself to become one with the fog.

On his fringes, he sensed that Bel and the others were close to the edge of the door, and he gathered, thick and soft, around the slumbering guards.

Cass was screaming now, inarticulate—terrified. "Boy! You buggering cunt—get back here! I'll teach you to fear, you sniveling cockroach! I'll rip yer prick off and shove it up yer nose!"

Harry ignored him, concentrating instead on the fine particles of mist his body had become, on the rolling waves of consciousness that held him together. He encircled Cass, thick, sentient tendrils of mist, liquid enough not to break as Cass thrashed against him, solid enough to bind him, hands to his sides, as helpless as Harry and Edward had been, as helpless as Francis had felt.

I have no fear of you, he thought, his mind slipping seamlessly into Big Cass's. He saw nothing there—void and fury, inarticulate rage. Perhaps there was pain—the ripping, raping kind—with no kindness after to temper it, but it was so long buried under the pustulating crust of bloody violence that Harry could no longer separate the wound from the wounder—nor did he care to.

Big Cass had two lifetimes to heal his wounds, to learn from his mistakes, to find another path. He'd chosen instead to continue hurting as he'd been hurt, to traffic in human flesh, to violate, demean, to kill.

I have no fear of you, Harry repeated. *You're small. You're an infection. You're the tiniest, most bitter parts of the human heart.*

I was your world! Big Cass howled. *I was the monster that made you gnaw at your heart for years! I was so huge in your heart you resurrected me a hundred times, brought me back to life by your need for a bogeyman—how can I be nothing now?*

I've been loved, Harry said simply. *I've brothers who would die for me. I've parents who've given me nine lives. I have a lover….* For a moment the mist wavered, and Cass thrashed.

Suriel! Holding Harry tenderly as they slept. Face slack, ecstatic, as Harry thrust hard into his body. Regarding Harry through liquid brown eyes as Harry fed him a minnow.

Suriel. Begging Harry to live.

Harry's soul drew a breath, and he remembered the one thing he absolutely could not do.

I have a lover, he said strongly, as the mist of his soul firmed up, became real. *Such a lover—our hearts in the night make a thunder that can drown your pitiful screams any day. I can't hear my fear over the sound of our lovemaking. There* is *no terror being held in his arms. I fear—oh yes, I fear. I fear never seeing him again. I fear losing him for the span of the world and heavens combined.*

But you?

You're a speck.

If you had me naked and howling under you one more time, you'd still be nothing more than a speck, a fucker, a rust spot, a bit of corruption on the skin of the planet.

I'll never fear your like again.

Big Cass screamed, the sound muffled in Harry's mist, and his body shook, shimmered, came apart—but not in gobbets of flesh, like before. He was, in fact, nothing more than Harry's imagination, his fear, his terror at being helpless, at not having a place to run.

At having a black hole where his faith should be.

Those things paled in comparison to Harry's fear of never seeing Suriel again.

They flickered.

Dissolved.

Rendered themselves unto mist.

Harry's mist.

The ringing of Big Cass's death scream wasn't even loud enough to echo in the warehouse cavern. Harry rolled out of the dark, festering building, leaving behind six sleeping guards and a floor scoured clean of every memory of Bel, the girls, and Big Cass.

He became cat at the door and trotted off into the sunshine, where his parents were waiting, and his brothers, and twenty grateful women who hadn't been victims in the warehouse—would never be victims again.

As soon as he cleared the doorway, he was forced to face Emma with her hands on her hips.

"You said we could fight," she said plaintively.

Harry changed forms. "There are six sleeping guards and a still-functioning human trafficking ring," he told her shortly. "Is that not enough fight for you?"

She scowled. "But Leonard and I were supposed to—"

Harry grimaced and tried not to be defensive. "He was *my* fear, Emma."

"He's not the only bad guy out there, Harry. From all accounts, he looked to somebody else."

Crap. "Well, we can hunt down his boss—but Cass was mine. My fear. My bogeyman. I needed to dispel him or we'd be fighting him into the next century. The rest of it, you can help with."

Emma rolled her eyes. "We can help with that? Oh, that's good of you. So kind."

Harry regarded her levelly until her lips twisted and she patted his cheek.

"Who told you it was time to grow up?" she asked softly.

"It's only been a hundred and forty years. Was about time, you think?" He sounded cocky, but he swallowed in sudden nervousness. Was this the moment— a hundred and forty years of being her boy— now that he'd conquered his fear, learned how to love, was this when he became too old to be her family?

She shook her head, her blonde hair falling forward into her face, reminding him of the young and desperate witch who'd summoned an angel and a demon in a clearing so long ago. Reminding him of a young, strong woman, in love.

"You still need raising yet," she declared. "Don't worry, Harry. I'm not going to kick you out of the house because you lost your fear."

He allowed himself a rare smile. "Good—because that's probably my biggest fear of all."

"Really?" she asked, her gentleness almost his undoing.

He looked away. "I can't talk about that yet," he rasped. "Do you and Leonard want to debrief the guards?"

"In a moment. How did you get rid of Big Cass?"

Harry felt a cruel curl at his lips. "Melted him into fog," he said with satisfaction.

Emma's warrior expression was most impressive. "That's my boy. Now, if you don't mind, yes—yes, I *do* think I'll have a go at the guards. We need the name of the leader here, because this thing they just did? With hunting down the ones that got away?" She bared her teeth, and if Harry hadn't loved her for so long, he would have been terrified. "This cannot be allowed to happen again."

Of course, she wanted revenge too—and Leonard did as well.

Edward and Harry both turned human and took turns giving the girls cell phones to call their families. Anya, in particular, wept on both of them.

"You guys—you have no idea. I just kept thinking about John and Krista, and how freaked-out they'd be."

"They were," Harry told her. It was important—John and Krista were found family, and Harry knew from experience sometimes you just needed reassurance. "They contacted us at our last drop-off. The family's been looking for you for—"

"Six days," Edward said softly.

Suriel had been dissolved before Harry's eyes little more than a day ago.

"It probably feels like forever," Harry told her with some passion in his voice.

"John talked to you?" she asked perceptively.

Harry looked away. "Yes—it's been a while."

"You broke his heart."

Oh Lord. "I was in love with someone else," Harry said, finally honest about it. "I couldn't give him what he wanted, even for a short time, if I was in love with someone else."

Anya's mouth twisted, and she leaned her head against his shoulder. "He figured. I just mean… he talked to you. He went to visit you and the family. He really must have been worried."

And this Harry could say without reservation. "More than you know. Krista is going out of her mind too. Your little family—it doesn't work without you."

The words mocked him. So easy for him to say to Anya, but his entire family had needed to intervene for him to understand them for himself.

"Remember when we did this four years ago?" Anya murmured. "I thought I had no one waiting. It's amazing how less scared I am, now that I know someone's out there who wants me too."

Harry swallowed and nodded, longing for Suriel a knot in his throat. Edward was still passing around the cell phone, and Francis and Bel were under the car, grooming each other unmercifully. For a moment it was enough just to hug Anya and give thanks.

EMPTY SPACES

EVENTUALLY THEY chartered a bus and used it to get everybody to Vegas. From Vegas, friends, boyfriends, girlfriends, parents—every girl had *somebody* worried about her who came to take her home.

Harry thought that if anything was a testament to the work his family did, that alone would be it. Every girl had family. Every girl was loved.

Bel and Francis never left each other's sides—they practically sat on each other in the car—and Harry asked himself and Edward repeatedly, how could they have missed this?

Finally Edward burst out with, "I don't know, Harry—maybe they were just born in love. You ever think about that?"

Harry blinked and tried to remember the first moment he'd known he was in love with Suriel.

And couldn't.

"No," he said, puzzled and wondering. "Is there such a thing?"

They stood outside on a balcony overlooking the strip in all its gaudy painted glory, and Edward sagged against the wrought iron, his own pain more than enough to destroy him.

"There must be," he said after a fraught moment. "You and Suriel, me and Mullins, Francis and Bel—we had no more choice or chance with the men we loved than we had to resist Emma, you think?"

And for once, Harry's reasonable, rational brother sounded young and lost. Harry rubbed a circle on his back. If they were cats he'd be grooming Edward's ear. "I think you're right," he said with a crooked smile. "But if you like, don't think of it as something we were powerless against. Maybe think of it as a gift. A reward, perhaps, for taking our lives and making good."

Edward cocked a skeptical eyebrow. "That almost sounds like a man with faith."

Harry's comfort motions stilled. "I have to," he told Edward in all honesty. "If I have no faith, I'm screaming in a corner." He swallowed hard. "So I'll have faith."

Edward turned and caught his hand, lacing the fingers tight. "Then I will have faith with you, brother. Because screaming in the corner is no way to pass the time."

They grinned tiredly at each other and then let go and turned back into the night.

Harry felt an insistent throb under his breastbone, like the pounding of surf.

Oh, how he longed to be home.

WHEN THEY finally pulled into the driveway of the big house, Harry and the others didn't ask permission. They waited for Harry to open the door as the car rocked to a final stop and followed him out into the green meadow surrounding the house in their four-footed forms.

Emma and Leonard would probably go inside and shower—and hopefully make love—but the boys had their own way to recover from a long trip.

Usually they hunted for hours, stretching cramped muscles, letting their brains take a break from the constant pressure, the constant fear of letting down the people they'd sworn to protect. Harry pitied the poor mice, voles, and jackrabbits that got in their way then. Sometimes they were creatures of violent anger, anger much more suited to a hunting house cat than a full-sized man, and they all knew that.

But today Harry had eaten his fill of rage, was sick to death of violence. Today he wanted one thing and one thing only.

Without looking to see where his brothers had buggered off to, he went trotting toward the cabin, out of sight of the house proper, toward the swimming hole.

Memories assailed him with every step.

155

The wrongness of traveling this path without Suriel by his side almost stopped his heart, and he broke into a gallop to get to the cabin. What if Suriel had been returned? What if he was injured, bleeding? What if he needed his boy?

Harry turned human just long enough to burst through the door.

The cabin was dark, as it had been when they'd both awakened. Their dinner dishes still sat in the drying rack, and Harry imagined their leftovers—chicken and rice—would be still in the refrigerator. Hell, it was only three days ago—they'd probably still be good.

Like he and Suriel would be eating them for breakfast the next day.

He looked around, at a loss. He'd helped build this cabin—it was only half a mile from the house. Get caught out in the rain? Visit the cabin. Get tired after fishing? Sleep there instead.

But now it was a different place. He walked to the bed, pulled the comforter to his face, and breathed deeply.

It smelled of eucalyptus and tea.

He sat down hard on the bed with a little moan and breathed Suriel in again and again, every lungful feeling like broken glass.

Every lungful like oxygen, necessary to live.

He hardly noticed when Emma and Leonard came in, sitting quietly on either side of him until Emma wrapped her arm around his shoulders and pulled him into her arms.

"He'll come back," she promised softly.

"Oh God," Harry wept. "Oh, Emma… I need him here. I need him. I need him. I need him…." Harry's breath caught in his throat, and he was sobbing, shaking with grief, and only Leonard's weight at his back and Emma's soft strength at his front kept him from flying apart like Big Cass, the ache of loss in his chest the biggest fear of them all.

HE FELL asleep between his parents, like a child. When he awoke, he was in his own bed in the house. Edward sat at the foot of the bed, a Kindle in front of him. Every now and then, he'd move his ginger paw, the Kindle would flash, and he'd turn the page.

Computers had made reading in cat form *so* much easier.

Harry pushed up to his elbow and frowned. "How long was I—"

"It's the next morning," Edward said, human now but not shifting position. He looked up from his book. "Emma is cooking enough food for a small nation. You'd better eat it."

Harry racked his brains, trying to remember when they'd eaten last.

"The gas station outside of Vegas," Edward said, like Harry had spoken out loud. "You ate then for fuel, and then let the girls eat the rest your food. Very noble, brother, but you're looking peaked. It's pissing me off."

Harry smiled slightly. "You are perpetually pissed off. This doesn't bother me."

Edward rolled his eyes. "Just eat, idiot."

"Yeah, sure." Harry pulled back the covers and discovered he was in his boxers. He felt the small smile before he even registered why it made him happy. "We'll always be their children, won't we?" he asked, knowing the answer. "Remember—when it first started? We talked about how we'd know when to walk away? How we'd know when it was time to not be Emma and Leonard's anymore?"

"Yeah." Edward sat up and stretched, both hands on the bed, arching his back and then flattening against the mattress. "We knew very little."

Harry had to laugh. "Very little indeed."

Edward stood upright and continued his stretch, his abs forming a perfectly corrugated washboard. Harry had a thought—probably long overdue.

"How come you and me never...." He made vague gestures with his hands, because even the question seemed obscene.

Edward laughed, unperturbed. "Because. You, me, Francis—we were all reborn that night we met Emma. We were brothers from the very beginning."

"Oh." Yes. That made perfect sense.

"What are you going to do?" Edward asked, exhaling and lowering his arms to his sides with the grace of a ballerina.

"You mean... now? Or until...." Until Suriel returned?

"Well, now. We don't have any missions to run. Emma and Leonard are still gathering data on Big Cass's friend. He's going to be out for blood, I think—the two of them were connected at the ball-joint, if you know what I mean."

Harry snorted. "Subtle, Edward. Real fuckin' subtle. But yeah. I think he'll be out for—"

"If you say 'pussy,' I will hurt you."

A real laugh this time. "No. No, I swear I wasn't going to. I was just going to say he's going to be gunning for us. We should watch out."

Edward nodded, smiling happily. "Now see—that's some common sense there, brother. I've been waiting years for that. So yes, there will be other missions, but not now. What do you want to do now?"

Harry thought yearningly of the cabin. "I'd like to... to build another cabin."

"Because you despoiled one and need to do that again?"

Harry hit him in the face with a T-shirt. "No, you wank. Because I want to *live* in the one. If... when Suriel comes back, I want to live there. So we can, you know...." Oh, embarrassing. Harry had gone *years* without talking this much.

"Be with family but have your own tiny, tiny space without internet or television or—"

Harry had to laugh. "Yes, we'd put those things in. But see? That's even more to do. But first, the family likes the cabin. It would be nice to not take it away."

Edward nodded enthusiastically. "Then I shall draw up plans!" he crowed. "Two cabins. Hell, we're on thirty acres." His face took on a half-hopeful, half-secretive look he often wore when thinking about matters of his own heart. "One for you, one for me, one for the family—"

"Not Bel and Francis?" Harry asked.

Edward laughed and spread his arms. "Bel's his mother's child, Harry. He gets this house, with his parents." His laughter faded. "After he gets back from Oxford."

Harry grimaced. "Oh Lord. Think we'll see more than the fur on Francis's tail between now and then?"

Edward regarded him kindly. "We pulled *your* head out of your ass—we can do the same for him."

And for once, Harry felt optimism flooding him, from the pit of his groin to the tips of his fingers. "We can indeed," he said grandly.

Fall....

"GO TELL her," Leonard said, wiping his brow in the early fall sunshine. "She needs to hear it from you."

Harry grimaced. "But she knows. I told her when she picked it ou—"

Leonard shook his head. "Months, Harry. Three months, to be exact. You and Edward showed us the plans for this place, she said, 'I'll decorate!' and I have heard about *nothing* but wall color, bedding, the right paintings, the right tile—three months. Every night—you want to know what my nights sound like?"

Edward was applying the last bit of sealant to the bright blue siding, and he snickered so hard his brush spattered.

Leonard was undeterred. "I fell in love with that woman because she talked about science and politics and literature—but not for the last three months! For the last three months it's been 'Do you think Harry will like this tile? How about the carpeting? Is the bathtub big enough? Suriel might have wings when he comes back!' Three months, Harry. I love you, son, but if you don't go in there right now and tell her she's brilliant, I may have to curse you."

Harry laughed heartily, storing the hurt about Suriel's wings away in his heart until later.

His family had worked so hard.

He and Edward had announced their plans for the new cabin that morning, and suddenly, instead of worrying about the future, instead of missing his lover with all his soul, he had something to do to fill the time.

Bel had been chivied to Oxford a month ago, but not without giving Francis an extraordinary, knee-melting kiss and a promise to write, real letters, not just email, every day.

Bel had been missed—so missed—but Francis, instead of spending his time catching mice, had been as invested in the cabin as Harry had.

The cabin was hope.

The cabin was a new beginning, a relationship that had waited nearly a century and a half to ripen and bear fruit.

Every nail, every board, every brush of paint, every speck of drywall—all of it was the brothers' willingness to believe they could be as happy as Emma and Leonard. They just had to have some faith.

It was bigger than the little fishing cabin. It had a guest bedroom and a study, for one. Leonard, ever the progressive thinker, had wired it for Wi-Fi, internet, and satellite—all pirated from Harry didn't want to know where, of course—and Emma had made it… a home.

The bed was handcrafted. Leonard and Bel had made it before Bel left. Emma had worked for a month on the quilt—red-gold, blue, but trimmed with black—and she'd put those vibrant colors all over the cabin itself. The bathroom tile was that deep, sea-crested blue. The moldings were the red-gold of Suriel's hair. Detailing—spellwork, for safety and welcome, Harry had read—in the finest, most perfect black adorned all the entryways, the closets, the kitchen, the bathrooms.

Friends or family would be welcome there. An enemy wouldn't be able to enter.

With every board and every detail, Harry built more firmly on the hope that Suriel would return.

"Yes, of course," he said now, walking away from the cleanup Francis and Leonard had started, stacking supplies in the back of the battered pickup truck Leonard kept on the property only. The thing was ancient, but Leonard maintained it using a combination of sorcery and mechanic prowess to keep it running.

As he opened the door and ventured into the shady, cool interior of the cabin, he heard Leonard swearing at the beast in Latin and assumed today, he would be using sorcery.

"Emma?" Harry called. "Emma?" He looked around, holding his arms wide and taking in the whole, perfect effect of it. "Emma, it's beautiful."

Emma walked in from the bathroom, wiping oil paint off her hands with a rag that smelled of turpentine.

"It is," she said happily. "I do nice work."

So much for her needing his opinion! But still, "You do indeed." He bit his lip. "I'm almost afraid to stay here," he murmured. "I want him to see it perfect, before—"

"Before your dirty boots mess up the floor and you spill something on the bed and forget to clean the toilet for a week?" Emma laughed. "No, Harry—you two, you'll be making it perfect together. You need to stay here." She bit her lip, suddenly no longer celebrating. "You need to have a space to pull him back to earth."

Harry blinked, the great wide space in his heart suddenly opening up, raw and bloody. "You think that's how it will happen?"

She nodded. "Given everything we know about how he left, what sort of trials he'll have to endure—yes. His love for you is his lifeline back to earth, Harry. You'll need to be in your place to pull him to you."

Harry bit his lip. "Will it be worth it? What he has to—"

She shook her head. "Don't doubt it, Harry. Don't ever doubt. This cabin is an act of faith. Believe."

He smiled and looked around again with appreciative eyes. "It's beautiful, my family's faith," he said after an aching moment.

"My sons are beautiful and deserve every scrap of it." Keeping her hands away from his shirt, she stood on tiptoe and kissed his cheek. "Now let's get back to the house so we can move some of your clothes in after dinner."

Harry's stomach rumbled, and she grinned.

"And maybe some provisions for you too."

EDWARD DROVE him back in the pickup, under a sky promising rain. The ancient vehicle jounced along a path carved by frequent trips in the past few months, and although noises had been made about at least graveling the road, everybody had been too excited about building the cabin to worry about niceties.

Edward pulled to a halt in front of the door, and they both looked curiously at the place in the darkness as silence descended.

The stream was less than thirty yards beyond the back door, but in the muted moonlight, all they could see was the ominous looming of the forest. The cabin itself was a dark L-shaped little building, its sprightly blue shingles turned gray by the night, without a thing to light it from inside, showing good intentions.

In the temporary hush, they could hear the surf booming. Harry had chosen a spot downstream from the other cabin, closer to the cliffs. They were maybe a half mile to the west—close enough to visit on even a rainy night.

"Don't haunt the cliffs like a romance hero, 'kay?" Edward said into the silence.

Harry turned and grinned, as though sitting on a promontory and letting the wind tease his whiskers hadn't been part of what he'd imagined for his nightly routine.

"'Cause that would be silly," he said with a smirk.

Edward didn't smile back. "You've been very optimistic these past months, Harry, and I know you're in it for the long haul. But…." Edward bit his lip. "I hate to think of you out here alone. Waiting."

Harry swallowed. Out here, away from the family he'd lived for. That had sustained him.

"Well, you're welcome to use the guest room. Emma did it in green."

Edward nodded. "I brought a change of clothes. Let's get your shit unloaded first."

He swung out of the cab, and Harry half laughed before following him. Oh, heaven bless his meddling, practical, sentimental brother.

In the months that followed, Edward and Francis would come out to the cabin to crash in his guest room many times. They'd track dirt over the floor, spill sodas on the bedding, leave handprints on the walls.

Every night, Harry closed his eyes and prayed.

He asked for Suriel back.

Winter….

"GODDAMMIT, HARRY!" Edward's voice, full of panic, drifted above him. "I thought we were over this shit!"

"I wasn't trying to get hit," Harry mumbled. It was true—this entire venture, from Sacramento to Canada, Harry had been the watchword for caution. But this organization was big, it was well funded, and Harry had been riding cleanup, fourteen scared girls into a van, Francis driving.

The bullet ripped through his arm and into his chest before he even knew they'd been flanked. Harry had toppled into the van with Edward screaming "Go! Go! Go!" and… he'd sort of lost track of things after that.

"I'm trying to stay alive," Harry mumbled, needing Edward to believe him. "'S why Francis is driving."

"*Drive faster!*" Edward screamed, and Harry let out a sigh.

"Feels like we're closer to home already," he said, because breathing had become easier, like they were nearing Mendocino and he was perched on the cliffs, the salt air setting his soul free.

"No!" Edward cried out tautly. "No. Not closer to home. Dammit, Harry—we need you! Didn't you learn that? *We need you!*"

"I don't want to leave," Harry said dreamily. "Promised Suriel…."

He closed his eyes and remembered that last moment, Suriel in the darkness, his smell washing over the both of them, the heat of their lovemaking still heavy in the air.

"Harry!" Suriel cried, sounding desperate. "You're not supposed to be here!"

Harry's eyes flew open. He was surrounded by a perfect meadow, one that smelled of hemlock and redwoods, skunkweed and salt water, with wildflowers floating on long green stems. The sun shone down in dazzling gold, and the earth kneaded warm beneath his toes.

His beloved stood before him, shackled to a tree, his hands swollen and purple over his head, perfect pale skin oozing blood from lash wounds all over his body.

"Well, neither are you," Harry said crossly, anger surging through him for the first time since Suriel left. "Why are you here? You're *supposed* to be down on earth with me, keeping me out of trouble!"

Against all odds—against *everything* the two of them had endured—Suriel smiled. "That was the plan. But you need to be down there to pull me to you, Harry, or I'm stuck here, suffering for eternity."

Harry growled. "This is bullshit. *What are you suffering for?*"

Suriel's smile grew gentle. "Same thing you're suffering for, Harry. I'm the bound angel. I suffer for those on earth who are bound against their will. If I'm to break my bonds, I need to suffer long enough to know my freedom for the gift it is."

A surge of blood flushed under Harry's skin. His breath came in heaving, searing gasps, and his brothers were calling him home.

But he hadn't seen Suriel in half a year, and he was damned if he didn't get in the last word.

"I'm your gift, goddammit! Get off your knees, break your chains, get down to earth, and love me!"

A gray mist obscured his vision, the heat of the sun fading, the smell of his beloved meadow becoming a memory of human sweat and exhaust. The last thing he saw was the unlikely image of Suriel, battered, lashed, starved, and bound, tilting his head back and laughing in delight.

His body was a misery of fire and ache, and breathing was a luxury, as distant as the meadow where an angel stood bleeding.

"Harry, are you with me?" Edward's voice held tears in it, and Francis kept up a hideous nonverbal yowl in the far corner of his mind.

"I'm alive," Harry croaked. "Francis, for fuck's sake, shut up."

The yowling stopped, and Francis shouted, "Don't do that to us, you asshole!"

"Sorry," Harry wheezed. The earth heaved and jounced underneath him, and he realized they were still in the van, and Francis was driving like a thing possessed. "Had to talk to Suriel. Stubborn fucker."

"Oh, of course," Edward muttered bitterly. "We're so blessed you came back from that."

"Well, *I* thought so," Harry grumbled. Darkness encroached again, but this time he was pretty sure he was only passing out.

The next twenty hours were a misery of bodies stuffed in a van, his brothers' irritated worry, and pure physical discomfort. But Emma had been spellcasting over their bodies for a long time, and Suriel had added his own protection in the quiet dark of the cabin. Unlike the wound Suriel had needed to heal, this one was not nearly as grave.

The only reason he'd ended up in heaven this time had been pure yearning to see his lover—but, like he'd said before, not a willingness to die.

Emma met them in Portland, and she and Edward spent an anxious night in a tiny hotel boiling herbs over lit candles, wrapping poultice after poultice over Harry's wound before digging the bullet out. The next day, Leonard took over the driving so they could move the girls out. Edward and Francis left Harry reluctantly, but Harry knew the score—the victims came first.

Yes, he was pissed at Suriel, his willing bondage, his suffering, being torn from Harry's side. But that didn't mean he didn't understand the nature of the higher calling. Resent it? Absolutely.

But oh yes—he did understand.

Understanding did not make healing any more comfortable.

Hell—*healing* didn't make healing any more comfortable.

When he was down to clean bandages and feeling like he'd been hit by a truck instead of mangled in its gears, Emma put him in the Cadillac and took him home.

He spent a week in the big house proper, watching as Francis and Edward decorated their world in pine boughs and tinsel while Leonard studded tiny LED lights throughout their endeavors like stars.

Harry—under strict orders not to move—was consigned to the couch to watch the frantic activity. Francis, in particular, moved with fever and intent. Bel was coming home for the holidays.

Leonard—finished with the lights and willing to let Emma trim the rest of the tree with purple ribbons and set out the knickknacks—brought him a mug of hot chocolate and company.

"You've been quiet," he observed after Harry sipped appreciatively.

"Punctured lung," Harry told him, although they both knew that wasn't the only reason he hadn't been speaking.

"Edward said you were speaking to Suriel when you passed out."

Leonard was such a plain man, average, comfortable. Harry was so grateful for his stolid kindness; he couldn't even imagine what it had taken for this man to sink into a world of torture and depravity.

For the first time, he wondered.

"I saw him," Harry confessed. He'd told nobody of this. "I saw him, in a meadow much like ours, being tortured so he would appreciate the taste of freedom."

Leonard grimaced. "You know, there was a reason I chose the other side." He shook his head. "But enough of that. Are *you* okay?"

Harry smiled tiredly. "Faith," he said softly. "Hope. Belief. They're not just words, Leonard."

Leonard nodded and gazed fondly at his wife, the woman who had pulled him from perdition into love, as she snuck just a little bit of magic to tie a bow on the part of the garland the boys had hung out of her reach. "They never were."

At that moment there was a knock at the door, and even Harry's wounds were forgotten.

Bel was home, and it was time for his family to celebrate.

THAT NIGHT, Harry lay in his old room, plain wood and rustic quilt, much as it had been for over a hundred years. On a whim, he closed his eyes and let his magic wander, counting the heartbeats around him.

Leonard and Emma, quietly talking. Edward, meditating on what Harry didn't want to know. Bel and Francis—oh my!

Harry pulled his attention from Bel's room in a hot hurry, stumbling instead on another heartbeat, frantic and thready, a man running for his life, mortally wounded, on his last hope.

Suriel!

Suddenly, suffocatingly, he was surrounded by the will of an angel striving with all his might to be free.

Suriel! Suriel, I'm here!

Harry—I can't see you! Harry—I need you—please—

Harry sat up in bed, reaching with his mind, his power, his heart, and his soul, trying to break through the barrier of the simple room into the dimension where his angel struggled against chains to find him.

The image gave him strength, and in his mind's eye he saw his fist punching through the barrier between earth and heaven, reaching for his lover in succor.

Then Suriel grabbed his hand back.

Augh! The pressure dragging Suriel away pulled mightily, almost ripping Harry's arm from its socket, reopening his half-healed wound, and his scream resonated in both worlds! Oh God, Harry was losing him, his life, his beloved, ripped away from his arms before he even had a chance to—

Help me!

In his heart, he called upon his family, and like a surge of adrenaline, they were there.

All of them, strengthening his magic, strengthening his body—his hand tightened on Suriel's and his magic opened, and together, he and the people he loved yanked with all their force.

The snapping of shackles ripped audibly through the house, and Suriel's exultant scream of freedom rocked the floorboards. Like a baby sliding from the womb into the air, Suriel ripped through the barrier between heaven and Harry and crashed into Harry's arms.

For a moment, Harry lay crushed, staring up at him in shock from his pillow while a naked Suriel stared back.

As they stared, the pain that had dogged Harry since he'd been shot warmed, eased, and health flowered up through his lungs, healing completely.

And the lashes that had scored Suriel's face healed almost completely, leaving only the faintest of silver scars in their wake.

"You still have angel magic," Harry said, stunned.

A slow smile blossomed over Suriel's pointed, lovely features. "And you're still brave."

Harry wrapped his arms around Suriel's shoulders and laughed and wept together, while Suriel did the same. That's where they were when the door flew open and they were suddenly surrounded by brothers and parents, all celebrating that their family was together—and it had grown.

Eventually the others went back to bed, leaving Harry and Suriel alone on Harry's narrow bed. Harry laid his head on Suriel's chest, stroking gently.

"What happened?" he asked softly.

Suriel's laugh held very little humor. "Have you ever heard the term 'a hell of your own making'?"

Harry pushed up on one elbow and searched his face. The scars were all but completely faded, leaving a bare suggestion of silver in their place, but his angel was leaner, worn, and sharp after his absence.

Harry's heart squeezed tight in his chest.

"What was your hell?" he whispered.

Suriel nuzzled his temple. "You," he whispered back. "I'd wanted you for so long. And I'd taken you—stolen time away from the world just to have you to myself. It was too much happiness for an angel used to being bound to service, Harry. I didn't feel worthy of it. I didn't feel worthy of you."

Harry sat up and smacked him, the tears spilling over. "Ass. Hole." He wiped his eyes with the back of his hand and flailed for words that wouldn't come. "How could… how could… how could…."

"Sh… sh…." Suriel sat up and folded Harry in his arms.

For the first time Harry noticed the absence of wings.

"Your wings…," he cried. "How could you—" He ran his hands blindly over Suriel's shoulder blades, feeling the scars he'd known would be there.

"I had to sacrifice something," Suriel said, his voice twisted. "I couldn't stay away from you another breath, another minute, not after you appeared before me so close to death. But you understand? I took joy in my work, Harry. I felt like I was giving to the world, sharing that terrible burden for all who were bound. I couldn't leave—not without giving something back, something to help those bound withstand their suffering. Do you understand?"

Harry nodded against his shoulder. "You gave your wings," he rasped. "Your great bird—?"

"I'll never fly again, not like that."

The grief in Suriel's voice nearly cracked Harry's heart in two, but then he remembered the healing. Suriel hadn't lost all his gifts—perhaps...?

"Your cat?" he begged, raising his face to his lover's in hope.

Suriel's smile was as pure and unfettered as it always should have been, without a trace of sorrow, not even for wings. "How could we live side by side if we could no longer fish for minnows?"

"How long?" Harry asked, thinking of extended lifespans, how his body showed barely ten years of a hundred and forty, and how Emma looked to be in her late thirties when he'd gathered she'd lived more than five hundred years. How long would he be forced to wander the earth, holding on for the time when he could see his beloved again?

"I have as long as you have," Suriel told him, tracing delicate fingertips along his hairline. He sobered. "So try not to make any more trips to heaven before it's your time, yes?"

Harry couldn't stop sobbing.

Suriel hushed him, kissing his face, his jaw, his ears, his neck, until the need for comfort dissolved, became a craving for touch, became *want*. Harry's sobs of breath turned to panting arousal, and Suriel's hands cruised his skin in discovery. He growled in disapproval when he found new scars and hummed with each cut of muscle, each sweep of unviolated skin. Harry thrashed beneath him, his grief, his joy, his fear transforming him to an open nerve and mindless frenzied arousal.

"Hold still," Suriel commanded, holding Harry's wrists above his head. "I need... I need inside you. You're my haven, my home. I need you around me."

Harry nodded consent, drawing his knees up, spreading his thighs. "Lotion's on the... ah!"

Suriel lowered his head, taking in one nipple, then the other, keeping Harry's hands suspended so he wouldn't flail. Harry keened, bucking his hips, lost in mindless need.

Suddenly his ears popped.

Suriel looked at him with wide, expressive eyes, and Harry took stock of where they were.

"My cabin." He chuckled, still mad with desire. "My bed. Guess we got loud."

Suriel's low laugh did nothing but stoke him higher. "Lotion?" he asked, a little desperately.

"Better. *Lube.* Under the pillow—" He freed his wrist from Suriel's and rooted for the little bottle he'd used to remind himself of this moment right here: Suriel's hands on his body.

He fumbled the bottle into Suriel's hand, only to be brought up short by Suriel's amused expression.

"What?"

"You were touching yourself." Reverence tinged every syllable.

"Uh—"

Suriel closed his eyes and breathed lightly through his nose. "I can almost smell your desire...." He opened his eyes again, his stare penetrating through the intimate dark. "Oh, Harry—the things you and I will do...."

Without warning he let go of Harry's wrists, placed both hands on his hips, and took Harry's throbbing erection into his mouth in one smooth stroke.

Harry's scream of arousal was probably *still* heard in the big house, but he couldn't have stilled it if he tried.

"So... oh God, Suriel!"

A small climax spurted hard into Suriel's hot mouth, but as Suriel parted Harry's thighs even farther, his arousal didn't flag.

Suriel's fingers, slick, nimble, probed at his entrance, and he buried his hands into that comforting fall of hair, thrusting against the back of Suriel's throat.

"Please," he whimpered. "Slow later. I need you now."

Oh yes! Suriel's body covered his, warm and sleek, the drive into Harry's entrance smooth and powerful. Harry sheathed him, aching with the stretch, and he cried out, filled.

"Oh yes," Suriel breathed. "Needed this. Needed *you.*"

Harry pulled his knees up, wrapped his ankles around Suriel's thighs, and urged him faster. Harder. Begged Suriel to drive him out of his mind.

Glorious! Suriel thrust, the sound of their flesh slapping filling the room, an animal thing, carnal and sublime.

Harry's body filled, not just with Suriel's cock, but with the enormity of his love, the great and terrible price Suriel had paid for this moment here, to be buried in Harry's flesh and held next to his heart. The knowledge swelled in his chest—swelled in his cock—and he cried out, the flash of light climaxing behind his eyes greater than human, greater than magic, somehow this animal act becoming the fulfillment of the divine.

Love in all its greatness was a truly heavenly thing.

Harry screamed, orgasm washing over him like the feeling of light spilling from his eyes, his fingertips, his cock. But only the feeling.

They were men, together, in love. When Suriel shouted above him and spilled into his body, the only thing that spilled from either of them was sweat and joy and come.

Suriel collapsed on top of him, laying little kisses on the side of his face, smoothing his hair from his eyes.

Harry smiled up at him, limp and sated and needing him all over again.

"That was only round one," he said, satisfied that they had all night.

Suriel smiled, all smugness and arrogance. Harry hurt with loving him so hard.

"We'll have to sleep sometime," he murmured.

Harry raised up to kiss him, taste him again, feeling Suriel swell while still in his body.

"Not yet," he murmured as Suriel began to rock back and forth again.

"Not yet."

FINALLY, OF course, they did sleep, and then they showered and ate, Harry feeding Suriel pieces of chocolate pancake across the table.

"So what now?" Suriel asked when they were mostly full.

"Christmas is tomorrow," Harry told him. "I'm sure Edward will be by with the truck in a couple of hours to come pick us up so we can spend it with family."

Suriel looked stricken. "Don't you give gifts?"

Harry regarded him steadily. "Are you going to make me say it?"

"I'm your gift," Suriel said, his smile a gift in itself.

"Oh yes," Harry confirmed. "That you are."

Suriel's smile faded. "But… I mean, the rest of our lives. However long that may be."

Harry shrugged. "I'm not tired of the family business just yet. You?"

Suriel frowned in thought, and for a moment Harry's heart failed him, and he imagined having to leave his brothers alone as they ventured into danger and into the rest of their lives.

"No," Suriel said softly. "No. That would be great, in fact. It's like continuing my mission here on earth. Gives me purpose." His thoughtfulness lifted. "Besides making love to you, of course."

Harry winked. "Of course." And then he grew thoughtful in turn. "My brothers aren't settled yet," he said baldly. "Edward—he's venturing into dark magics. If he and Mullins don't solve what's between them, like you and I did, I fear for him. Not just his body, Suriel, his soul."

Suriel nodded, looking grieved. "Yes, I can see how that could be worrisome. And you're right. You and Edward have always needed each other. I wouldn't take you away from him. Certainly not now."

"Good." Harry swallowed. "Thank yo—"

"No thank-yous. I loved you all, Harry." Delicate color danced over his pale features. "Just, you know. Not the same as you."

Harry bit his lip, shy in a way that surprised him. "That's, uh, good to know," he said with dignity, and then grew serious again. "And Bel and Francis are…."

"Still lovers?" Suriel asked anxiously.

Harry didn't color—he blushed. "Oh my God, yes. But they're not settled either. Bel leaves and Francis turns inward, all cat, all skittish. He needs to find himself before he and Bel come together for real. They haven't even told the parents yet."

Suriel frowned. "Do Emma and Leonard know?" he asked.

Harry shrugged and nibbled pancake thoughtfully. "It's possible. Emma knows everything, usually, and Leonard only pretends to be the distracted father. But—" He grimaced. "—I needed them. They'll need—"

"Us," Suriel said, putting a syrup-sticky finger on his lips. "They'll need us. I'll never desert you again, Harry. That means being there for your brothers, for Emma and Leonard, even for Mullins, because he's loved your family too. Don't worry. I didn't escape my bindings because I disliked being bound by my word. I escaped them because I wanted to choose who I'd bind my life to."

Harry smiled then, and licked his finger. "Me, right?"

Suriel laughed and traced his lips. "Idiot."

Harry sucked his finger into the cavern of his mouth, and Suriel tilted back his head and closed his eyes. "Think we can go again before Edward gets here with the truck?" he asked seriously.

Harry released his finger and grinned. "I think it's worth the try."

They were barely done and barely dressed by the time Edward and Francis knocked on the door. Suriel made the bed while Harry washed the dishes, chivvied on by his brothers about being lazy and not doing his chores.

Harry gave back as good as he got, but inside, he was thinking of magic.

And how you didn't really have to be an angel to fly—you just had to be in love with one.

Harry planned to fly with Suriel for centuries to come.

AMY LANE is a mother of two grown kids, two half-grown kids, two small dogs, and half-a-clowder of cats. A compulsive knitter who writes because she can't silence the voices in her head, she adores fur-babies, knitting socks, and hawt menz, and she dislikes moths, cat boxes, and knuckleheaded macspazzmatrons. She is rarely found cooking, cleaning, or doing domestic chores, but she has been known to knit up an emergency hat/blanket/pair of socks for any occasion whatsoever or sometimes for no reason at all. Her award-winning writing has three flavors: twisty-purple alternative universe, angsty-orange contemporary, and sunshine-yellow happy. By necessity, she has learned to type like the wind. She's been married for twenty-five-plus years to her beloved Mate and still believes in Twu Wuv, with a capital Twu and a capital Wuv, and she doesn't see any reason at all for that to change.

Website: www.greenshill.com
Blog: www.writerslane.blogspot.com
E-mail: amylane@greenshill.com
Facebook: www.facebook.com/amy.lane.167
Twitter: @amymaclane

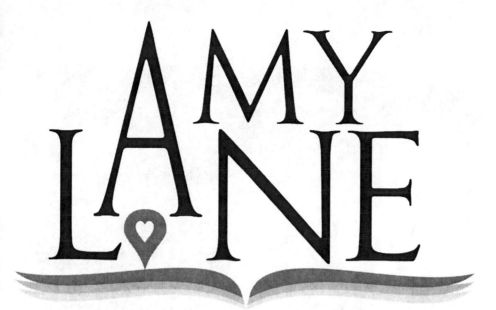

Choose your Lane to love!

Purple

Amy's Alternative Universe Romance

Dreamspinner Press
Fairy Tales

HAMMER & AIR

Amy Lane

There will always be a Hammer and an Air...

Graeme and Eirn have no words for what they are to each other. Children, clinging together in a crowded orphanage; friends, battling back to back in a school yard; and bedmates, finally bridging the gap between sleeping next to a body and allowing it to touch you in the night—all of these roles are summed up by just their names: Hammer and Air.

The innocent exploration of their newest roles is brutally marred when a violent, ill-tempered master threatens Eirn, and Eirn's "Hammer" kills the man in a fair fight. The two run off into the wide world with only each other for safety. It's difficult to forge a good life with only a blacksmith's hammer and a printer's cleverness, but together, Hammer and Eirn will learn to negotiate the dangers of magic and motion, of sex, obsession, and tenderness, and of the word that can make sense of it all—one word they must earn for themselves.

www.dreamspinnerpress.com

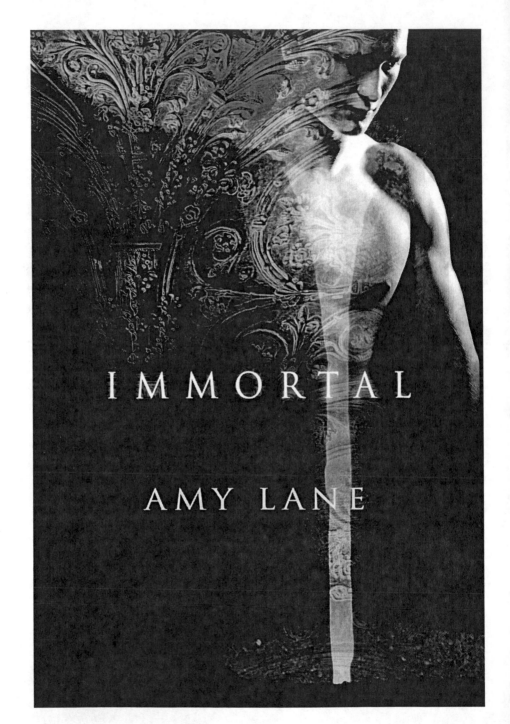

IMMORTAL

AMY LANE

When Teyth was but a child, a cruel prince took over his village, building a great granite tower to rule over the folk. Greedy and capricious, the man will be the bane of Teyth's existence as an adult, but as a boy, Teyth is too busy escaping his stepfather to worry about his ruler.

Sold into apprenticeship to the local blacksmith, Teyth finds that what was meant as a punishment is actually his salvation. Cairsten, the smith, and Diarmuid, his adopted son, are kind, and the smithy is the prosperous heart of a thriving village. As Teyth grows in the craft of metalwork, he also grows in love for Diarmuid, the gentle, clever young man who introduces him to smithing.

Their prince wants Diarmuid too. As the tyrant inflicts loss upon loss on Teyth and Diarmuid, Teyth's passion for his craft twists into obsession. By the time Teyth resurfaces from his quest to create immortality, he's nearly lost the love that makes being human worth the pain. Teyth was born to sculpt his emotion into metal, and Diarmuid was born to lead. Together, can they keep their village safe and sustain the love that will make them immortal?

www.dreamspinnerpress.com

AMY LANE

A SOLID CORE
OF ALPHA

In an act of heroism and self-sacrifice, Anderson Rawn's sister saved him from the destruction of their tiny mining colony, but her actions condemned the thirteen-year-old to ten years of crushing loneliness on the hyperspace journey to a new home. Using electronics and desperation, Anderson creates a family to keep him company, but family isn't always a blessing.

When Anderson finally arrives, C.J. Poulson greets him with curiosity and awe, because anyone who can survive a holocaust and reinvent holo-science is going to be a legend and right up C.J.'s alley. But the more C.J. investigates how Anderson endured the last ten years, the deeper he is drawn into a truly dangerous fantasy, one that offers the key to Anderson's salvation—and his destruction.

In spite of his best intentions, C.J. can't resist the terribly seductive Anderson. Their attraction threatens to destroy them, because the heart of a man who can survive the destruction of his people and retain his sense of self holds a solid core of alpha male that will not be denied.

www.dreamspinnerpress.com

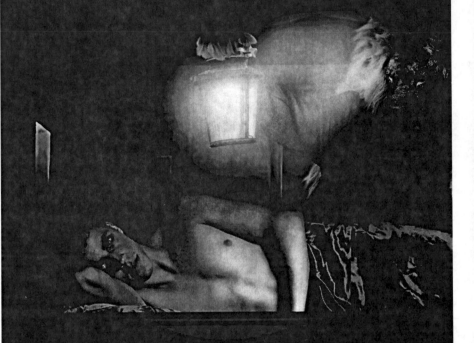

Truth in the Dark

Amy Lane

"I am not beautiful..."

Knife's entire existence has been as twisted as his flesh and his face. The only thing beautiful in his life is his sister. When Gwennie is obliged to turn a suitor down because she fears to leave her brother to the brutality of their village, Knife is desperate for anything to ensure her happiness.

Her suitor's cousin offers him a way out, but it won't be easy. Aerie-Smith has been cursed to walk upright in the form of a beast, and his beloved village suffers from the same spell. Aerie-Smith offers Gwen a trousseau and some hope, if only Knife will keep him company on his island for the span of a year and perform one "regrettable task" at year's end.

Knife is unprepared for the form the island's curse takes on his own misshapen body. In one moment of magic, he is given the body of his dreams—and he discovers that where flesh meets spirit and appearance meet reality, sometimes the only place to find truth is in the darkness of a lover's arms.

www.dreamspinnerpress.com

AMY LANE

UNDER THE RUSHES

Ten years after Dorjan trusted a boy's word over his superior officer's, he and his best friend, Areau, are still living the aftermath—and trying to stop the man responsible. Locked in a careful dance to bring down a corrupt government, Dorjan struggles to balance his grief with Areau's anger. Just when Dorjan reaches the end of his rope, he sees a familiar face in the shadows, and the boy he trusted a decade before offers him unexpected kindness.

Taern remembers the soldier who found him under the rushes and listened to his pleas to save his family. When Dorjan reappears in his life, Taern is both captured by his commitment to justice and terrified by the risks he takes. All Taern wants to do is fix him, but the oncoming destruction has been ten years in the making, and Dorjan doesn't want his help. Not if it puts Taern at risk.

Powers clash and a world's fate dangles between Areau's madness and Dorjan's nobility. While Dorjan fights to save the world, Taern joins the battle simply to save Dorjan, knowing everything hinges on the heart of a man in armor and the strength of the man who loves him.

www.dreamspinnerpress.com

CPSIA information can be obtained
at www.ICGtesting.com
Printed in the USA
FFOW02n0019200917
40146FF

9 781635 339451